For every woman who flourished despite the people that raised her.

SPEARTIP BREACH
ESAKLI CITADEL
ESKALI FJORD
STARBORN GLADES
WAR CAMPS
RYDAR
STARBORN
SILVER ORE PORT
DISTANT SHORES
BURNE'S SECRET
SILVER SEA
SILVER COAST
GAZAR
GREY JUNGLE
GAZARI PORT
CAPE OF CASTREL

Sapphire Mines
YORE
Port of Yore
Forgotten King
GHOST LANDS
LDS OF FALLEN
THE WINTER WILDS
THE CLANS
WAR CAMPS
THE BLACK ESTATE
THE BLACKWOOD
BRILEND
BRULA
BRULIAN PORT
THE BRIARWOOD
THE FROZEN SHORE
CALOS VALLEY
PORT OF CALOS
SVALTA

CHAPTER 1

ELEANOR

Eleanor's grandmama always told her she was a reckless girl, and that her wandering heart would lead her into trouble.

She was right, as grandmothers usually are.

Now Eleanor was nothing more than a discarded fruit. Not ripe or shiny enough for a man of worth. Love was a rotten, mealy apple and it ruined her.

"You're really throwing me off with the apples." Mary paused in her scrubbing to wipe her brow. "Is love the apple? Or are you the apple?"

"Neither! Both!" Eleanor smacked her brush down onto the stone with a wet slap. It echoed through the empty dining hall, rebounding into her like a cracking whip. "What I am is soiled and unwanted, Mary. Perhaps I was born that way because my own parents cared so little for me that they dumped me with a wizened old woman."

"Oh, not this again. You spend too much time feeling sorry for yourself, Ellie. So, you laid with a man? Everyone does it. Even high-born ladies do it. They'll tell you they don't, but I've seen 'em. I once walked in on Lady Bertrand on all fours with her skirt lifted, while one of the cooks went at her. Virtue and purity are a load of horseshit."

Eleanor gasped so hard she inhaled bubbles. "Lady Bertrand? With who?"

"Arnold."

"Arnold? But he's so ornery and stout."

"He is stout indeed." Mary pointed her finger and propped it between her legs in a vulgar gesture. "I wouldn't mind him having a go at me."

"Mary! Gods! I can't believe you."

"What? If men can walk around putting their cocks in anything warm and wet, why can't women seek a bit of pleasure? You don't even have to love the man. It's usually better if you don't." She dipped her scrubbing brush back into their bucket of hot water and sloshed it around. "Was it really your first time? What were you saving yourself for?"

Jerome. "Nothing in particular."

"Well, was it worth all this talk of rotten apples, at least?"

Eleanor chewed her lip, tasting the mingling of sweat and soapy water. "He will never take me as a wife nor be proud to have me at his side." A tear slipped down her cheek, though she promised herself she would shed no more for him. "I thought he loved me, Mary."

"Oh, sweet Ellie." Mary abandoned her brush in the bucket and wrapped wet arms around Eleanor. "You're too soft hearted. He doesn't deserve to have you."

"I didn't deserve to have him. He's betrothed and now I have taken something from his bride. And it was for nothing! He made me believe we could be together if only I would give myself to him."

"Pig!" Mary snorted. "Who is he? Tell me and I'll be sure to throttle him."

"You can't, Mary. No one can know I was with him."

"He's that close to the crown?"

Eleanor glanced over her shoulder to see that they were alone. The dining hall was empty, dull light filtering in through the narrow windows to reflect onto the stone floors. Above them, the high ceiling made sound bounce oddly between the wooden rafters and back down to where they scrubbed beneath the tables. No one was in sight, but anyone walking down the adjacent halls would hear scraps of their words.

Eleanor cupped a hand around her mouth and whispered, "He will wear the crown someday."

———◦◆◦———

HUMILIATION PAINTED ELEANOR'S FAIR skin a shade of red so vibrant she matched Diana's fuchsia gown. It was just her luck that Diana noticed, pausing as she snatched a teacup from Eleanor's tray and sneering at her. "What's the matter with you? Your face looks redder than that awful mop you call hair."

Eleanor was no stranger to taunts about her hair. As a child, she'd come to hate the color and prayed to the Gods to change it. Make it a brilliant red or a pale blonde, not the strange in between that it was. The other children teased her, saying she couldn't even get being a ginger right. She was often asked if she was born with red hair, but her mother confused her with a cleaning rag and dipped her in a tub of lye.

"Changing your hair wouldn't make you comelier, girl. Ignore those brats. Half of them will die before they're old enough to wed anyway," Grandmama snapped whenever Eleanor came home in tears. "A poor woman doesn't have the luxury of worrying about her peers. Soon you'll need to put food on the table. I can't have you wasting your time pouting over hair."

So, Eleanor didn't pout or defend herself, only bowed her head and murmured, "It's warm today, my lady."

"That's *princess* to you." Diana was not the princess, nor would she be for many months, but that didn't stop her from throwing the title at her lessers whenever she pleased. "Are servant girls all this stupid?"

Eleanor wasn't supposed to be here. Her task was cleaning, and she did it well, scrubbing floors, dusting, and picking up after the slobs that called themselves royalty. When she agreed to take the place of one of the girls from the kitchen, giving the poor creature a respite from the stairs as her belly—and her feet—grew more swollen by the day, Eleanor thought she was meant to serve the queen. The queen was always entertaining company with tea and cookies.

If she'd known she would be waiting on Jerome and his betrothed, watching the too familiar touches between them, she would have chucked the tray and gone home.

"Come now, my sweet. Quit fussing over the help and give me your lovely company." That voice. Gods, he was so refined. Charming and quick to pay compliments.

Eleanor struggled to keep her eyes from him as she stood there with her tray, waiting to be dismissed. Prince Jerome was classically handsome. His hair was the perfect shade of brown—like shined chestnut—and his blue eyes were intelligent and bold. The cut of his jaw gave his face just the right amount of angle to appear masculine, but not harsh.

Her gaze drifted to his hands—soft for a man's. She was intimately acquainted with those hands and the rough way they gripped her hips as he thrust into her. Jerome lifted her skirt with an expertise she should have been wary of. He hadn't prepared her for his entry, nor cared that she was in pain.

"It's to be expected for a maiden. Widen your legs. That's right. Now beg me to take you."

She could live with that dreadful part of the memory. Mary assured her that no woman enjoyed it the first time. It was what he did after that would leave a permanent scar on her heart.

Jerome laughed at her.

Eleanor sat up, pushing her skirt down to hide the blood between her legs, and confessed her love for him.

Stuffing himself back into his pants, he chuckled. With that sound, the charming lover was gone. He eyed her coldly, asking, "Surely you didn't think I cared for you? You're just a maid! A maid with the best tits I've seen in a while, but too lowborn for me to look at you when I'm not fucking you."

The greatest feat of Eleanor's life was holding in her tears as he snuck from the closet they met in. The final words Jerome tossed over his shoulder broke her hold on her emotion. "Meet me here again tomorrow. I want to know what those lips feel like around my cock."

For once, she was relieved that Diana made a surprise appearance. It saved Eleanor the trouble of avoiding the prince and his wrath—for now. She hadn't thought love could be so complicated. Nor had she believed Jerome to be such a cruel, fickle man. Grandmama was always warning her that she trusted too easily.

"Jerome!" Diana pouted. "You haven't even told me that you like my new gown. I had it made just for you."

"Forgive me, Diana. I was too distracted by your beauty to notice your gown. It's lovely. The color suits you." The color was hideous, so in this case, he was right. "I could ravish you right here in the library."

"Oh Jerome! How improper. Before the wedding?" She pressed a hand over her mouth and whispered, "Whatever would people say?"

"Just a little ravishing then?" He held his thumb and pointer finger up, a familiar determination set in his features. Eleanor was going to be sick. "You there! Run along, servant girl. My betrothed and I require complete privacy."

She quickly obeyed, clutching the tray so tightly that she thought it would break. What a womanizing scoundrel. Eleanor *hated* him, absolutely loathed his very existence. And she couldn't work in his castle for another moment. Maybe she wouldn't even stay in his *country*! Far to the south, Calos recently gained a new queen who was rumored to be lenient and kind, building a better world for women like Eleanor. She was a dragon bride too—the first in half a century—and the creature kept her kingdom safe.

Calos was a very, very long trip from Brula. She would have to travel over two mountain ranges. First to reach Dunhill, then to the southern peaks that overlooked Calos Valley. Dunhill had its own trouble with dragons, or so she'd heard. Recently, a princess was snatched away by the beast that lurked in their expansive forests. Eleanor wasn't clear on whether she was ravaged or ravished. Mary told her it was both.

"Dragons are violent lovers," she explained. "They can't exactly be tender, what with all those teeth and claws."

Eleanor shuddered at the thought of a woman lying with a beast. Living with one though—hidden away in a dragon's cave and spending the rest of her day isolated from everyone—sounded preferable to her current existence. She was a good cook and an excellent maid. All the qualities a dragon would need in a human wife. She was no longer a maiden and in stories, dragons always stole maidens. Perhaps one would make an exception for her if she was especially useful to him?

Brula was a small country, but their dragon population was larger than most. She'd never seen the family of dragons that lived cliff side by the frozen shore. Their existence was mostly ignored by Brulians. They didn't steal maidens, to Eleanor's knowledge, nor did they eat people and slaughter livestock. A wealthy family in that region paid tribute to them each full moon and that seemed to keep them at bay.

The same could not be said for the dragon that soared over the Winter Wilds beyond the Brulian capital. One evening Eleanor snuck into a guard tower to watch him take to the skies. Truly a breathtaking creature. He was unruly though, making a raucous noise most nights. For some reason, the sound of him made her feel unbearably sad, like the weight of her lifelong loneliness grew heavier. It was one of those sounds that reminded her of some distant memory that she couldn't quite place. Melancholic nostalgia.

The dragon was still on her mind as she wandered from the castle and through the streets of the capital. Grooves were carved into the road where carts and wagons had sloshed through the wet ground before the freeze. It would be rough and hard to navigate until the spring melt softened the hard packed dirt enough to rake it. Wooden buildings, glowing from the inside out with fire light, stood sentinel on either side of the road. Their snow crusted roofs made them look like aging men to Eleanor.

A thousand scents hit her as she entered the bustling town square. She tried to focus on the warm bread, stewing meats, and spiced wine bubbling over a fire rather than the acrid stench of frozen piss and un-washed bodies. This was the wealthier part of the capital, where lords and ladies would walk carefully along the cobblestone path beneath the awnings of shops, studying fine fabrics and nibbling pastries, but the folk that lived here weren't that much better off than the rest of Brula.

Only royalty had the luxury of hot baths and plumbing. The rest of them had to make do.

Merchants pushed carts through the streets, singing praises for their wares. Eleanor was paid a fine enough wage working in the castle, but she didn't have much to spare. Enough to feed herself and her grand-mama and indulge them here and there. Today she'd been paid and decided they were long overdue for an indulgence. Eleanor stopped a plump baker whose cart steamed with delicious, sweet scents.

For Grandmama, she purchased a squash pie. The creamy orange flesh of a preserved autumn pumpkin rested inside a beautiful crust, sprinkled with warming spices. For herself, Eleanor selected winter-berry pie. The color was blood red and the flavor as tart as it was sweet. They were a rare Brulian treasure, only growing the few weeks before and after the winter solstice, and Eleanor cherished every taste of them she got. Grandmama had forbidden her from venturing beyond the wall to pick them in the Winter Wilds, but it hadn't stopped Eleanor from sneaking out and doing it anyway when she was a girl.

Now she hadn't the time and freedom for such rebellions and stuck to using her precious coin to treat herself. If she was a dragon bride, she could probably pick berries whenever she pleased. A wolf or a winter cat wouldn't dare eat her if she had a dragon at her back.

It was a silly and fanciful daydream, but after today's heartbreak, Eleanor was considering it. She wanted so desperately to run from the capital and never return.

Who would look after Grandmama, though?

"Where is it? Give it here!" Grandmama dropped her broom in the middle of the floor and ambushed Eleanor at the door as she walked in.

"For a wizened old woman, you're surprisingly spry," Eleanor teased. "Whatever are you pestering me for, Grandmama?"

"Don't play games, child. I could smell it before you walked through the door." She clapped her bony hands together, her tired face graced with a rare smile.

Eleanor shut the door to the cottage, pretending it did some good to keep the fierce cold out. This far north, the winters were truly unbearable. Her hands and feet were numb by the time she returned home from the castle, even gloved and stuffed into fur boots. Snow left her garments damp if she ventured outside too long, and the wind could rip right through her.

The hearth was the sole place of warmth in the entire single bedroom home this time of year and Eleanor often took to sleeping beside it. How her grandmama survived in that frigid bed each night was beyond her. The wooden walls were packed with moss and clay to insulate, and the round shape of the structure left fewer corners for draughts to sneak in but here on the outskirts of the city, where farmers and laborers called home, there was little protection from the elements.

Without the larger buildings like the shops in the square, the wind had free access to whip between houses. Though the towering outer wall loomed beyond the collection of cottages and barns, it could do nothing to protect them from the westward air blowing in from the port. Sea breezes were brutal in the winter.

"These old bones are decorated with hoarfrost," she once told Eleanor. "I was born on the coldest day of the year, and I will likely die on that same day. Winter bothers me none."

Eleanor emptied her sack on the table, laying out the pies and a bundle of nubby carrots. If she could afford to buy produce from one of the glass house farmers, they would be eating more than carrot and turnip soup for the next three months. But those coins went to fetching winter rabbits and the rare strip of elk meat to keep Grandmama fed.

"They've gone cold," she warned. "Shall I heat them first?"

"Who cares about cold!" Grandmama snatched up the squash pie and stabbed a fork into it, moaning greedily and stuffing several bites into her mouth at once. Eleanor was pleased to see her eating so voraciously. The old woman was looking thinner all the time and Eleanor feared a winter would soon come where Grandmama withered away completely.

Eleanor set her pie on an iron pan and used a tool to drag coals into the cooking pit. She set the pan on the coals and got to work cleaning carrots while the pie heated. The bucket of water she kept beside the shallow sink had a layer of ice atop it and she had to break it with her fist before dunking the roots. By the time she was finished, her skin would be red and her knuckles stiff.

"Why do you love those berries so, girl? My mother used to warn us not to eat too many or a dragon would smell them on us and snatch us away."

Strange, Grandmama almost never spoke of dragons. It seemed the creature was haunting her. "Dragons like winter berries? I thought they ate sheep."

"They like the smell. It reminds them of maiden blood." She licked her fork.

"That's morbid. I don't think they smell anything like blood."

"Not that kind of blood, girl." Another bite of pie. "The kind you only bleed once."

Eleanor froze midway through cutting a carrot, her hands going strangely numb. "I see." No dragon would care for her, then. She'd already bled her maiden blood.

"What's the matter with you?" She must have stopped longer than she realized. Grandmama had finished her pie and was moving about their tiny kitchen, preparing the onions for broth.

"Forgive me, I must be tired."

"Liar." Grandmama had a nose for dishonesty. "Was it talk of the dragon that made you wary? Or maiden blood? You'll bleed soon enough, girl. Soon as you take a husband like I've been telling you to."

"Who would take me as a wife?" she murmured.

"There's always the butcher's boy."

"He's still a bachelor for good reason."

"He can't help the way he looks any more than you can!" Grandmama dropped onions into an iron pot and began filling it with a pitcher of water.

Eleanor quieted. She knew she wasn't the most beautiful woman, but on today of all days, she wished her grandmama wouldn't be so blunt about it.

"That hair of yours will never be a good color 'til it's gone white like mine, and your freckles aren't becoming either. But you've got a healthy set of hips and a plump bust. So long as you can offer virtue and obedience, a decent husband won't be too hard to find." Grandmama continued as if they were having a two sided conversation. "You would contribute your fair share to this household if you could find a man to look after you. I never wanted you as a burden and I've cared for you long enough, I think. It's time you started caring for me."

Some days, Grandmama was kind to her. But more often she had bouts of anger, blaming Eleanor for all of her misfortune and unhappiness. She was an unwanted burden, a bastard soiling their family name. Though Eleanor spent her life trying to give back to her grandmama what she received as a child, it was never enough.

It wasn't enough that she found work in the castle and saved her spare coins in case Grandmama couldn't work the fields any longer and needed more help. It wasn't enough that she cooked and cleaned all day in the castle, only to come home and do the same. She chopped wood and fixed the roof during the wet months of summer whenever there was a leak, cleaned the chicken coop, and hauled water when the well wasn't frozen over.

None of it made a difference.

Feeling defeated and exhausted, Eleanor dropped her knife and turned to her grandmama, blurting, "I cannot offer a husband those things, so perhaps I will stay unwed forever."

Grandmama stared at her, the pitcher still tilted though it was empty. "You are an impulsive, worthless girl. Only the name you were born with made you anything of value, and even that proved fruitless." She smacked the pitcher down on the counter and shuffled from the kitchen. "I've been on my feet all day. I'm going to lie down while you finish the soup. Bring it to me when it's done."

Eleanor did as she was told, heaving the iron pot to hang on the rack above the fire. Her hands went from numb to scalding as the heat blistered her fingers. She dropped to the floor beside the hearth, staring down at those hands. They weren't soft or dainty like Diana's—not the hands of a lady. Callouses armored her palms and the ridges of her knuckles were rough and dry from the cold and the cleaning soaps she used. She hadn't been a desirable match before—fair, but spoiled by those blasted freckles that never faded when the summer months did. Unprepossessing features and a figure that was neither slender nor rounded and feminine.

She wished to be called plain, as Mary was, but her coloring was too specific. Plain, at least, would make her normal. Another of the hundreds of boring women who entered boring marriages of convenience and lead boring lives.

Now? Eleanor wasn't even good enough for that. One dalliance with a lecherous prince and she was ruined. No amount of plainness could save her from her own poor decisions.

Grandmama was right, she thought, stirring carrots and parsnips into the soup. Unkind in her delivery, but truthful all the same. Eleanor settled on her knees before the fire. She was filthy from her day's work and couldn't be bothered by the ash that soiled her dress. With those unladylike hands, she forked an even more unladylike bite of pie and savored the warmth and tartness on her tongue. The sweet was gone in six forkfuls and still her stomach rumbled for more.

In three weeks, they would celebrate the winter solstice. The castle would be alive with all the most important guests, and the kitchen would fill with the aroma of warm spices and savory meats. Winter-berries would be only one of many rare delicacies served to the lords and ladies of the court.

How was it that they came to sit at fancy tables and wear fancy clothes while servants brought them their every wish? Wealth and power, Eleanor was observing, were often accrued by those who worked the least in Brula. Many lords and ladies inherited their fortunes and had never worked a day in their lives for their worth.

Meanwhile, those that braved the Winter Wilds for berries and meat were paid copper for the enormous risk they took.

Gods, she hated sounding like a rotten child, but it wasn't fair. And she was so sick of it all—the stupid courtiers and their ugly sneers, the prince and his mask of kindness, the back breaking scrubbing and dusting and hauling of kitchen supplies. Each and every day she began her work before the sun, worked until it vanished quite often too. Yet she was filthy and unworthy. Courtiers passed her by with noses upturned as if she were an unsightly pest.

If all the *unsightly pests* were to march out the castle gate and leave the royal family to fend for themselves, they would starve in their own waste. Their ostentatious lifestyles disgusted her, so Eleanor supposed they were even.

"No more," she whispered to the fire. It had always felt especially comforting to her, an old friend who listened quietly and never spoke judgment. "I cannot take any more."

The fire hissed and crackled back to her, beckoning her closer. She had the strangest feeling that she could take it inside of her, burn from within and warm the frozen, bitter parts of herself.

Fire cared not for courtiers and counting coins to buy bread. It was wild, an untamed force that could be as merciless as it was merciful.

Eleanor chucked another log beneath the cooking pot. "Do you promise not to burn this place to the ground if I'm not here to tend to you?"

Fire could make no promises. It burned what it wished whenever it wished. The control man had over it was an illusion.

"I won't hold you to it," she told the fire.

Might serve Grandmama right if the house was devoured by flames because of her carelessness.

What a dreadful, dreadful thought.

Eleanor didn't take it back.

Chapter 2

Eleanor

THERE WERE ONLY THREE gold coins, six silvers, and twenty coppers in the pouch she kept hidden beneath her clothing chest. Grandmama couldn't lift it, so Eleanor knew it was safe there. To her, the pouch seemed heavy, her savings bountiful. Until she counted it, that was. Three was a measly number.

Eleanor must have been indulging them more often than she realized.

Regardless, three coins would get Grandmama through the winter and then some, so long as she was spending them wisely. Grandmama was never particularly wise with her coin, but that wasn't Eleanor's responsibility any longer. She would cease being a burden to her grandmama and in return, the sour old woman would do the same. Eleanor was an unwanted child and Grandmama cared for her out of obligation and fear of the Gods.

But the day Eleanor was strong enough to carry buckets and pull weeds, she was out to work. Grandmama cared for her as much as necessary to guarantee she wouldn't starve. Beyond that, she expected Eleanor to recoup the grief of raising her by pitching in her fair share. That fair share turned out to be less than fair as Grandmama aged. Eleanor couldn't begrudge her the pains of aging.

What she could hold against her was the gambling. The lengthy naps while there was garden work to do, and Eleanor was busy working in the castle. Many summer nights she was picking vegetables by moonlight and blindly wiping down the sides of the chicken coop with the hope no waste was left behind.

The hard truth she learned as she came of age was that her grandmama was not a motivated woman. Eleanor couldn't fathom why she agreed to take on the child of her worthless son. But she was grateful to have been raised to womanhood without abuse—physical anyway—and so she would care for her grandmama in their parting.

With care, Eleanor placed the coins on the kitchen table in a tidy stack. If she could read and write, she might have left a farewell letter. Or perhaps not because Grandmama was also illiterate. Earlier she'd brought Grandmama a serving of root stew and brought in another bundle of firewood so the old woman wouldn't grow cold when she rose late with the morning sun.

Leaving her family home should have felt more saddening. The journey she set out on should have filled her with more trepidation, too. Eleanor was not made with the sense of caution most people had. Nor was she particularly sentimental, having never felt that she belonged in this house or even in Brula. The Gods were clearly guiding her away from here and she was listening.

Even with all her winter layers—a fur lined cloak, fur boots, and knit wool gloves—the air was painfully cold. Though it was morning, the sun wouldn't rise for hours yet. To venture beyond the capital and into the Winter Wilds was dangerous business.

Eleanor wasn't afraid. She'd snuck her way around the outer wall many times and knew the edge of the forest intimately.

The wall was built from massive logs, hauled there by Brulian ancestors to guard the city from man and beast alike. Though the construction was skillfully done, the wood was grey and old, having cracked and disintegrated in places. Eleanor was familiar with several of those places, finding gaps just large enough for a large fox or a slender girl to slip in and out.

There were wolves to worry about—they were always the most ferocious in the winter months when prey was scarce—and snow cats, but they didn't often venture close to the city. The people of Brula were not vulnerable nor incapable. They hunted and foraged in parties, carrying sharp spears and bows. Eleanor carried neither, but it was her hope that the predators were accustomed enough to Brulian presence that they avoided her.

Snow crunched underfoot, punctuating her every move with that familiar winter song. The guardhouse at the outer gate was easy to avoid, and even if she walked right by it, the guards were too bleary in the early morning to hear her strutting along the perimeter of the wall. Hopefully, it was less penetrable from the outside.

Though, who would invade Brula? The country did well enough, but their ground was frozen most of the year, which made for poor crops and their most worthwhile export was fur.

None had been desperate enough to brave the mountainous terrain and weather yet. Likely, none ever would. Brula was the least interesting place to conquer, in Eleanor's opinion.

Exhilaration flooded her when she slipped through a thin crack in the wooden wall and stood tall under the trees. Most were free of leaves, their smooth trunks bone white. The unusual, bleached bark of the bonewood trees was what the Winter Wilds were named for. Even in summer, when their pale blue leaves were plentiful, the forest appeared ravaged by cold.

The further Eleanor traveled through the wood, the thinner the bonewood trees would become, giving way to spruce and varieties of pine that handled the high elevation and cold well. On her most rebellious and adventurous day, Eleanor ventured far enough into the wood to pick spruce tips. In the springtime they were soft and bright green, their flavor sweet and tangy. For a girl denied all the luxuries of the world, spruce tips were treasure. Tree candy, she used to call them.

That same day, she fell from a thin tree branch and sprained her ankle. Grandmama threatened a beating. Eleanor plied her with her satchel of fir tips. To this day, she regretted giving up her treat to save her hide. A beating was much more survivable than long nights with an empty belly and an appetite for sweets.

Winter left the sun dull and sleepy. He climbed lazily over the horizon hours after her departure, reaching golden fingers to the treetops. It was enough for Eleanor to see that she was indeed alone, and no predators lurked in the shadows, but not much more. It would be noon before the day wasn't gray and only if clouds didn't come to blanket the sun. Still, she marched onward through the snow, weaving between trees and keeping her eyes open for danger and delight.

With a gasp of glee, Eleanor dropped to her knees and embraced the evergreen bush she'd been searching for all morning. Her basket was large, but by the time she was done picking beautiful, plump winterberries it was overflowing. Juice stained her fingers and dotted the snow around her like blood spray. The berries exploded on her tongue, first sour, then sweet.

"Thank you," she murmured to the Gods.

Eleanor skipped through the trees for another hour, making little progress as she picked and munched on berries. It wasn't until she heard a familiar roar and the thump of wings beating the air that she halted in her tracks.

He was here.

Moments later a great shadow swept over her. Eleanor watched as the glacier blue belly of a dragon soared low over the treetops. His legs were tucked close to his serpent-like body. They were decorated on the ends with gleaming icicle claws. As he passed her, he roared again, louder and more insistently. She had the strangest feeling he was calling for someone.

Remembering herself, she shouted, "Wait! Dragon!" But the wind had picked up and his wings rustled the trees so violently, there was no chance he would hear her.

Eleanor began to run, her neck craned to follow the dragon as he quickly made his way further up the slope. Her breath was such a thick fog it nearly blinded her and more than once she almost ran into a tree. As the hill steepened, she began to slow. But she wouldn't stop. Determination kept her pushing through the burning in her thighs. She faltered only when her basket fell from her grasp and berries tumbled everywhere.

Conflict caused too much hesitation and the dragon gained a larger lead. Eleanor watched as he circled in the distance before diving somewhere out of sight. Good. He landed. Now at least she didn't have to run.

The berries were crusted with frost by the time she finished collecting them from the ground, as were her gloves. All that running had warmed her for a time, but her sweat was beginning to cool, and a bone deep shiver took her. Maybe the dragon would roast her. Compared to freezing to death, it sounded a pleasant way to die.

Eleanor wouldn't accept defeat, so she trudged on, tiring quickly as the hill seemed to become vertical. The distant howl of a wolf, answered by another that was much closer, put speed back into her step. Overhead, the sun was already wandering back to his home behind the peaks, yawning cool golden rays that scarcely made it through the trees. Another hour and it would be dark.

But Eleanor wasn't going to need another hour. Towering black rocks jutted above the treetops not two hundred feet before her.

Climbing from within the rock structure like smoke from a chimney came a massive steam cloud. *A hot spring.*

"Gods, I'm going to soak until I'm soggy."

She wasn't the only one with that plan. Teal water bubbled at the base of the rocks as she crested the hill. There he was lounging comfortably in the spring—*the dragon.* His scales shone like glaciers, his wings an icier color. By far, the most spectacular part of his coloring were his eyes. Those eyes with pin shaped pupils were the palest shade of blue she'd ever seen, nearly a match to the snow.

Coiled like a snake, the dragon appeared smaller than she expected. Not small the way a house cat was small, but not some gargantuan monstrosity either. Eleanor could probably straddle his back and ride him, though he didn't look as if he'd be too happy about it. That pointed snout was hiding a great many teeth, and those jutting icicle-like spikes atop his head could easily impale her.

Eleanor slowly set down her basket and travel satchel. Next, she removed her gloves and dropped them onto the ground with a wet plop. "There you are! I've been calling for you, dragon. Didn't you hear me?"

He blinked at her, raising his head slightly from the water.

"Clearly not. Anyway, I've found you now." Finally tasting some trepidation, she gave him a sloppy curtsy. "I'm Eleanor."

His entire body shifted this time, rising from the water to look down at her.

Grandmama was right. Eleanor could be so very impulsive. Now she was two dozen feet away from a dragon who suddenly looked hungry.

CHAPTER 3

VIGGO

THE WINTERBERRY GIRL WAS here. Standing at the edge of his pool as if she were an angel descended from the palace of the Gods. Viggo had begun to believe she was a figment of his imagination. Her scent would appear in faint wisps throughout the wilds just often enough to keep him searching. But when he called for her, she never came.

I've been calling for you, dragon. Didn't you hear me?

Neither of them had heard the other, it would seem. Viggo blinked at her, still not believing his eyes. Her hair reminded him of the strawberry frosting that decorated summer solstice cakes. Red diluted with sweet cream to make the prettiest pink color. And her skin was dotted with little marks like he'd never seen before. Were they *all* freckles? He didn't know a woman could have that many. Would she let him count them?

She was weighed down by a heavy winter cloak and many layers, but for some reason she was shedding them. Her nose was pink from the cold and her sweat had to be freezing on her skin. Still, she continued until he was convinced she would disrobe completely.

Why had she come to him now, after all this time?

Eleanor, she called herself. Eleanor was young. Not too young to wed. But perhaps she had been before. Perhaps she hadn't understood his call until she came of age.

Very well. He could forgive her absence then.

"You've got the right idea, dragon." Clad only in a worn dress, Eleanor stepped into the pool, moaning softly. As she grew near, he realized how badly she was shivering. Getting wet wasn't going to help her. She didn't seem to care. "I'm sure you're wondering why I've come all this way." A step closer and her heart began to pound. "Well, I have a proposal for you."

Viggo inclined his head, waiting for her to continue.

"I've come to ask you to take me as a bride." She smiled sheepishly. "I'm not a maiden but I can cook and clean. I'll be obedient and keep the dust off all your treasures. I think I could make an adequate wife, even if I'm not of good breeding or well educated." Eleanor curtsied again. It was clumsy because of the water and her stance. Her complete lack of grace was endearing, her manner refreshing.

But who had she lain with? He'd been waiting for her to come to him for years. There should have been no one. Viggo narrowed his eyes and huffed an irritated breath.

Eleanor's face fell and...were those tears? She wiped at them angrily, sputtering, "Fine! I know I'm a worthless girl and an ill match for anyone. If you won't take me as a bride, would you please just eat me? Swallow me whole and end me now. I can't take it anymore!"

What happened to her to drive her to beg a dragon to eat her? Viggo was intimately familiar with her pent up frustration. That was why he was here, living feral in the Winter Wilds. He couldn't take it anymore either.

Viggo tucked his head and began the shift that would put them on level ground. His body felt stretched in that comforting way a morning stretch eased sleep aches. Then he was shrinking down, coming lower and lower to the ground until he was only a foot or more taller than her instead of a dozen.

Eleanor's hazel eyes grew wider and wider until they were nearly all white. Her mouth opened, closed, opened again only for her to say, "huh?"

"Haven't you heard? Dragons only take maidens."

◆

ELEANOR

He was a man. *A man.* Eleanor shook her head, certain she was mistaken. But no, there he was in all his naked glory. And he was glorious indeed. She'd never seen a man fully nude before—unless she counted old man Lito and his rather public sunbathing—and hadn't realized they were so artfully crafted. Perhaps they weren't all built this way. Jerome definitely wasn't hiding that much muscle under his clothes.

The dragon man was tall—really, very tall—with thick arms, thick legs, and a thick...everything. His stomach was ridged and taut, scarcely moving with his breath. And that chest? Oh, Eleanor could lounge on that chest like one of the fainting ladies on chaise lounges in those dramatic castle paintings.

Beads clacked as he shook water droplets from his pale blonde hair. Its length could rival hers, coming down over his shoulders in a series of long braids. Sky blue beads decorated the thinnest braid coming off the side of his temple, the very same shade as his eyes.

Was he a God? He looked like a God. His accent was strange, as if he spoke the old language, and he could turn into a dragon. *A dragon.*

"Have you seen your fill?" He smirked, his high cheek bones accentuated by the expression. There was a taunting quality to his face and Eleanor got the impression he didn't take anything seriously. When she didn't immediately respond, he scratched his pointed jaw and flexed his arms.

"I may never see enough to have my fill," she answered honestly. "Are you one of the Gods? Have you come here to play tricks on me or get me with child?"

"No, perhaps, and definitely. We can begin practicing now, if you like."

Eleanor narrowed her eyes at him. "I thought you said dragons only want maidens."

His smirk fell away. "I prefer that no one has touched my things before I use them."

Without thinking, she splashed him. "Well, I'm not a thing to be used, so it seems my trip was pointless."

His jaw dropped and Eleanor feared he would cuff her. Lords often would if she did something wrong. A dragon had to be a step above a king or a queen. The dragon man surprised her by letting out a deep belly laugh. "You ran through the Winter Wilds after a dragon? Only to splash him in the face?"

"I told you I don't have good breeding or any of the manners that come with it." She crossed her arms and moved closer, mostly because the wind was freezing and so was she. "W-what are you if y-you're not a God?"

"Your teeth are chattering."

"O-obviously."

"I'll warm you, sweet little El." He purred invitingly and for a heartbeat she almost accepted.

"I've had enough of ch-charming men who w-want nothing more th-than a quick l-lay. I d-don't even know your n-name. And I thought y-you were a d-d-dragon." Eleanor scooted her feet along the slippery rocks until she was submerged up to her chest. Hopefully she didn't lose her footing because she wasn't a particularly good swimmer.

"Viggo." He growled a very dragon growl, those blue eyes lightening as his pupil shrank beyond what was human. "What *men* are you talking about? How many have you had?"

Eleanor was tempted to splash him again, but her arm was under water, and it was blessedly warm there so she left it. "That's none of your b-business."

"You offered to be my bride. It's very much my business."

Fair point. Was she still offering if the dragon wasn't a dragon at all? "There was only one man. I loved him but he ruined me, then cast me aside. I'm not some loose skirt, you know. I never would have…" she didn't want to talk about it, especially not with this stranger. *Naked* and very forward stranger. "It doesn't matter to you. I'm not a maiden so I'll finish warming myself and then I'll take my leave. I have somewhere to be, anyway."

He slid closer, looming over her. How was he so tall? Eleanor wasn't sure if she could reach the top of his head. "You're going to walk through the Winter Wilds, soaking wet? In the dark? Where do you have to be that's so pressing?"

"You're nosy."

"You're mad."

"Well, I'm glad I could amuse you." She turned to leave the water, knowing he was right and that it would likely be her death if she walked through the woods as she was.

But Eleanor didn't make it to the shore. One moment her feet were planted awkwardly on a stone, the next she was airborne and bouncing on a very muscular shoulder. Eleanor shrieked. Who would come help her out here? If anything, she was probably drawing curious wolves closer.

"Stop squirming and I'll fetch your things."

"And take them where? What are you doing, you brute?" She slapped his back, her hand making a wet clapping sound that made her giggle despite herself.

"My crazy El, quit wiggling." Viggo stopped to pick up her basket and her satchel. He left her winter clothes piled on the ground.

"I might need those! Where are you taking me?"

"To my home," he explained. "Didn't you learn anything about dragons before you came here? We snatch women and carry them off to caves."

"That sounds barbaric." She cleared her throat. "It's worse with you being a man, you know. A dragon couldn't do much but eat me. What is your plan? Are you going to make me bear your dragonlings?"

"Oh, yes," he teased. "All twenty-seven of them."

"I hate uneven numbers. It'll have to be twenty-eight."

They swiftly climbed past the hot spring, up the steep rock face. Even with her on his shoulder, Viggo was agile as he followed a narrow trail that seemed completely vertical at times. Eleanor squeezed her eyes shut as the spring shrunk to the size of a puddle far below them.

The wind suddenly died, and his footsteps echoed hollowly. Eleanor opened her eyes to find they were in a cave carved into the side of the rock. It wasn't particularly deep, but the ceiling was high enough that Viggo didn't hit his head. In fact, it looked the perfect size for a dragon.

"You have a lovely cave," she mumbled, feeling incredibly off balance and not just because he set her on her feet after hauling her up a cliff.

Viggo smirked. He seemed to do that a lot. "See? You have some manners." He sauntered over to a dark pit in the back of the cave, vanishing from sight. Then flames exploded before him, first blue then fading to red. He could breathe *fire*? Eleanor wished she was a dragon.

"Do you actually live here?"

"Are you having second thoughts?" Eleanor averted her eyes as he tugged on a pair of simple wool pants.

"I hadn't really given it any thought."

He stilled, his profile half lit by the fire. "None?" With two strides he was before her again, staring down at her with such intensity. "Why are you here, El?"

"*-eanor*. Eleanor." Why was she correcting such a silly thing? "I'm here to be a dragon bride. Or to freeze in the Winter Wilds and be reincarnated as a beautiful spruce tree." She stretched her arms over her head.

"You wish to die?"

"No." She considered. "But I wish to live a different life."

"And I am your escape." Viggo turned back to the fire, snatching a long stick from the pit and using it to light torches and candles placed in crooks and crevices along the walls.

"I thought you were a dragon!" Eleanor wasn't trying to be defensive, but she hadn't expected him to be offended. She hadn't expected him to be a man. "You still haven't told me what you are."

"*Drakonmein*." The word rolled elegantly off his tongue. "We are an ancient kind of shapeshifter, gifted our second skin by the Gods."

"The Gods gave you a dragon? They must like you very much." She rocked on her toes, feeling the cold seep back into her. "Why do you need a bride? You live in a cave. There isn't much that requires tending."

Though, as the fire illuminated the cave, Eleanor realized that wasn't entirely true. A wardrobe was propped up against one wall. There were barrels and crates of food stacked haphazardly in the corner. Just beyond the fire pit was a pallet layered with fur blankets and plush pillows. Other eclectic pieces dotted the space. Where did this stuff come from?

"Is that all you think a marriage is for?" He scooted a chair up to the fire and gestured for her to sit. "Come, you're cold. A good husband would strip you from those clothes and warm you the proper way." Another gesture, this time to the notable bulge between his legs. "A marriage isn't for finding a woman to dust and cook supper."

"It's about satisfying the urges of your cock?"

Viggo's brows jumped up his forehead. "Are you always this unabashed?"

"Yes. Grandmama says I don't think before I speak. Or act." Eleanor warily took the offered chair. She was freezing, her dress soaked and becoming a suit of ice around her.

"She's right." He dropped to the floor, reclining on a bearskin rug.

Eleanor expected a dragon cave to be dank and dark. She imagined there might be a pile of gold and jewels somewhere for him to nest in—dragons were rumored to love treasure. What she was seeing now was much more luxurious than expected. Not castle luxury, but enough fine fabrics and comfortable chairs to be curious. Did he steal furniture from lords and ladies, flying off with blankets and wardrobes in his claws? There were a great many questions Eleanor had for him.

"Yes, perhaps she is." With a deep sigh she perched her elbows on her thighs, leaning toward the fire. What a peculiar day.

"Tell me, El." Viggo shifted to his side, propping his head up on one hand and drawing circles in the fur beneath him with the other. Somehow that tiny movement was seductive, warming her in ways the fire couldn't. "Where would you go if you didn't stay here? What would you do?"

"I told you, I'll become a spruce tree. Or perhaps wander the Winter Wilds until I find a pack of wolves to join. Eat tree bark and become a wizened winter witch who devours children and speaks to spirits. I have plenty of options."

He studied her, lips pursed slightly. "Do you have a very bizarre sense of humor, or are you completely serious? I can't seem to tell."

That teased a small smile from her. "I'd say it's a bit of both. It's a joke if you want it to be. But if I can't stay here, I'll make my way out there."

"You won't return to your home?"

"No." Eleanor made her mind up and once she had, there was no changing it.

"You really want to be a dragon bride?"

"I wouldn't turn the opportunity down." The truth was that she would gladly accept a marriage proposal from the likes of him, even if he lived in a cave. He interested her and she had the feeling they could talk about anything without being shuttered by etiquette. Not to mention, his looks could rival a God and more than once she caught herself staring at his midriff and wondering if he would let her lick him. But she'd been too eager with Jerome, and he used that against her. Eleanor was wary of giving Viggo a chance to do the same.

"Not a maiden, no manners, and you sound as enthused to be my bride as a woman asked to clean the privy. Why should I accept you?"

She shrugged. "You don't have to. I've explained to you my better qualities."

Viggo grew quiet and went so very still. For some reason his eyes became like the dragon's again, a lighter blue with pupils long and thin. Eleanor held his gaze but the longer she did, the more she felt edgy. She wasn't sure if she wanted to run from him or crawl across his body. Fear and feral want were a confusing mix inside of her and she was too overwhelmed.

"Prove yourself to me. Show me your wifely skills. Then I shall make my decision." He rose from his spot on the floor, stretching slowly and letting each and every muscle on his stomach contract. Eleanor almost applauded him for his showmanship. Viggo knew that she was struggling not to stare at him in his half-dressed state.

Eleanor watched him pull back the blankets and slip beneath them, snuggling into the pallet and sighing. She glanced between him and the fading fire, feeling the cave cool again already. "And where am I to sleep if I stay?"

She couldn't see him, but she was sure he was smirking when he answered, "In our marriage bed, of course."

Eleanor stood, shaking. "I will not lie with you to prove myself!"

"No? Does a wife not lay with her husband?" That damned accent made every word a seductive purr.

"You haven't made me your wife." She fisted her hands on her hips. "I won't be taken advantage of."

"I wouldn't dream of it, sweet El. Now come to bed."

"No games, dragon. I won't allow another man to abuse my trust."

Blue glowed threateningly from beneath his lashes. "Your trust is safe with me."

Eleanor shouldn't have taken him at his word, but she was cold, and she felt inexplicably safe with him. A dragon! Turning her back to him, she quickly dug through her satchel for her spare dress—the only other one she owned. If she was to stay here, there would be no avoiding him seeing her immodest on occasion so she didn't hesitate before stripping from her wet clothes and redressing.

The side of the bed not occupied by him was cold, but the weight of the blanket reassured her that she would soon be warm. And—"Soft!

It's all so very soft. It's like lying in a cloud." She propped up on her elbow, searching for his face in the dimming light. "How do you get it so soft?"

"Furs above and below, bear mostly. It's quite comfortable, isn't it?"

"You have no idea." She flopped back onto the fluffy pillow, fluttering her legs beneath the silky inner sheet. "I sleep on the floor next to the hearth. It's not good on the joints. But this? I'll be downright springy tomorrow. I'll have energy for days!" Grinning, Eleanor flopped again until she was close enough to touch him. "I may very much enjoy my stay with you, dragon."

"I have a name, you know."

"Sure, of course. Sorry. Viggo. Dragon groom." She rolled over, nestling into the pillow and unashamedly scooting to soak up his body heat. There was no harm in that if he wasn't going to take advantage, was there?

Another of those rumbling dragon noises came from him and she couldn't hold in her giggle. "Sleep bride. We rise early tomorrow."

With a sigh, Eleanor obeyed, falling easily into the most comfortable sleep of her life.

What a very strange day indeed.

CHAPTER 4

VIGGO

VIGGO WAS EITHER DEAD or dreaming. She was here, in his *bed*. And sleeping as soundly as a child too. He shifted under the furs, moving as close to her as he dared without waking her. Eleanor was far, far too trusting. Or completely and utterly reckless. Perhaps she was both, and a little unhinged too.

He'd take an unhinged mate if it meant she braved the Winter Wilds to find him.

Only, she wasn't really looking for *him*. She wanted a way out of her predicament. After all this time she came to him and wanted nothing more than an escape. Fool that he was, he would give it to her. But what would it cost him to find a mate that felt nothing for him? He couldn't bond with her under these circumstances. It would spoil the beauty of that connection if they made it without both of them wanting it.

And she didn't truly want him.

Oh, she was attracted to him. That, at least, was obvious. Many women found him striking, though. What he desired was more than her desire. He wanted her dedication, loyalty, and love. Those didn't come overnight, he supposed, but it was hard not to feel impatient after all this time. He knew she was out there, scented her among the trees, felt the ghost of her presence, and searching for her nearly drove him mad.

Feeling bold, Viggo stretched his arm over her side and gently rested his palm on her back. She was cool despite the furs. It hadn't occurred to him that his humble home wouldn't be suited for a mate. Dragon brides were always ordinary women—his kind didn't pass their gift down to daughters—and they weren't as equipped to survive harsh environments. Had she left this evening as planned, Eleanor would have frozen to death.

Viggo moved closer still, and she did the same, turning to snuggle into his chest and burrow her face beneath his chin. Was this a cruel dream? Would he wake tomorrow to find his bed empty, his heart even emptier? So much time had passed since he first caught her scent that he'd begun to believe she was a creation of his mind to dull the endless, boring days.

He inhaled deeply, drawing her into his lungs. Winterberries, spruce, and something uniquely feminine. Exactly as she smelled that very first time. It was spring, and he was coasting over the trees, admiring the blue-green leaves of the bonewoods when it struck him. Faint but so alluring that his heart began to thunder. Viggo circled for hours, tracking the trail that weaved between trees. It must have been old when he discovered it, because it ended on the outskirts of the capital, muddied by the stink of the city.

For years he searched for her, knowing precisely who that scent belonged to. *Mate.*

He was as sure of it as he was his own name. But she never seemed to leave the city after that first encounter and if she did, it was only to hover along the outskirts. He thought he caught sight of her once, a slim figure slipping through a hole in the outer wall, but she didn't come when he called to her.

In his family there was a myth about mates and dragon calls. His father always insisted a mate would know the call of the *drakonmein* meant for her, as his mother had. Clearly it wasn't always the case.

Sleeping, Eleanor appeared so soft and youthful. Her skin was flawless and taut, dotted with sweet constellations of freckles. With her lips parted she reminded him of one of his mother's prized works of art, a fallen angel lamenting her descent from the heavens.

"Beautiful," he whispered, taking her hand and kissing it. The skin of her palms was rougher than he expected. What kind of life did this strange woman lead?

"Don't fuss, I'll put another log on," she murmured, slipping that hand from his and patting his side in search of a nonexistent hunk of wood.

"No, I'll do it. You sleep."

"Mmm. Thank you." She nestled deeper into his hold.

Viggo closed his eyes, focusing all his energy on his body heat. She wouldn't need a fire now that she had him.

———◦———

E LEANOR

They didn't rise early, as Viggo promised. For the very first time in Eleanor's life, she was allowed to lounge about in bed, keeping the same morning hours as the sun. What she hadn't expected was that Viggo would do the same. She also hadn't expected to wake up touching him.

One side of Eleanor's body was chilled despite the heavy furs, cool and clammy the way she always was when she didn't wake to tend the fire at night. The other side was so wonderfully warm that she thought perhaps the fire had tiptoed from the embers in the fire pit and crawled into bed with her.

"Hello, good friend," she murmured to the fire, shimmying closer and tightening her arm around its waist. And what a good waist it was. Trim and firm and too smooth to be clothed. Fire probably didn't have a need for clothing. "Thanks for keeping me warm."

"Isn't that a husband's responsibility?" A deep voice purred.

Eleanor's eyes opened as wide as they could. The fire in the pit was gone and the dull grey of winter dawn was not enough to light the space. Even so, Viggo's half-dressed body wrapped around her was unmistakable.

"What are you doing, scoundrel?" She swatted his arm away and rolled from bed. Immediately she regretted it as the cool air hit her like a battering ram of ice. The cave blocked the wind, but it did little else to provide sanctuary from winter's torment. "I was very clear, sir dragon. I will not lie with you."

"Unless I take you as my bride?"

"We can negotiate then," she chattered, searching hopelessly for fire starting tools. "W-where do you keep your f-flint?"

"I don't." He was a monstrous shadow looming over her as he rose from the bed, prowling like an animal to the fire pit before sucking in a deep breath and coughing out a quick spray of sparks.

"Can you make it bigger?"

"You'll have to add logs." He gestured to the pile.

Eleanor took one and carefully placed it beside the fresh sparks of life he'd given the embers. "No, I mean when you breathe it. Can you breathe a big cloud of fire like when you're the dragon?"

Viggo chuckled and pulled a shirt over his head. "Have I impressed you, El?"

"*Eanor*. Eleanor. You can't just go around changing people's names whenever you like." She all but stuffed her hands into the flames when they finally caught. "Is this your only source of heat?"

He had the decency to look apologetic. "I'm afraid so."

"Very well." She steeled herself for a miserable day. It wasn't much different than working in the cottage. The only warm room was the kitchen. "I'll warm myself with work."

There turned out to be quite a few candles littered about the cave. Eleanor counted more than twenty as she flitted from wick to wick, quickly lighting them before her twig burned too low and singed her fingers. By the time she was done the sun was a subtle white glow behind the clouds and the cave was beautifully illuminated.

The illumination was the only beautiful thing. Now that she could see it clearly, the furniture obviously needed some mending. Cushions on plush chairs had stuffing spilling out in claw shaped lines. There were two questionable stains on the lounge nearest the entrance that could be blood. And the dust. Gods, the dust. How did he live here without sneezing constantly?

By the time she'd made a round about the space, she'd sneezed half a dozen times. "When did you last clean?"

"Clean?" Blue eyes gleamed with amusement. "I've never cleaned."

"Clearly." With a huff she pushed up her sleeves, twisted her hair tightly on top of her head, and began searching for the supplies she would need to make the cave livable.

An hour later Eleanor paused in her dusting, dropping the scrap of fabric she'd found in a corner filled with crushed furniture and random objects to wipe her brow. Her stomach rumbled angrily, and she thought longingly of the winterberries from yesterday. They were notoriously bad for keeping and needed to be baked or preserved as soon as possible.

"You're hungry?" Viggo sat by the fire, arms crossed, and legs propped up on a crate of empty mead bottles. She was beginning to suspect that dragons were lazy. Perhaps a dragon wasn't a good choice for a husband. Grandmama always warned her that a lazy husband made for a miserable wife.

"How can you tell?"

He tapped the side of his ear. "I can hear your stomach."

"That's embarrassing. What else can you hear?"

That smirk was back. "Just about everything."

Eleanor glanced at the collection of rusted cast iron in that dreadful pile of junk and sighed. "How do you cook? I see no usable cookware and nothing to make the fire manageable for food."

"I've never cooked," he admitted, looking sheepish. "It's easier to eat as a dragon."

With a frustrated grunt, Eleanor dropped beside the fire and flopped onto her back. Her back would be coated in dust when she stood, especially because she'd worked up quite a sweat. "What exactly do you do?"

"I spread my wings, search for the nearest elk—moose if I'm especially hungry—and snatch it in my claws. From there it's fairly easy to—"

"No, Viggo. With your time? What does a dragon do with his time? Are you a scholar? Do you steal treasure to hoard?" She glared at one of the wrecked chairs. "Real treasure?"

He shrugged. "Sometimes I read. I like to go flying. There are plenty of hot springs to swim in and the wilds have many places to explore."

Eleanor covered her face with her hand, saying a prayer for patience. "Nothing of importance then." Was he just another version of Jerome? A man who worked little for all that he had and shirked his responsibilities in pursuit of pleasure? "It's come to my attention that

I need to inquire more about your lifestyle. I fear I may be more suited to become a spruce after all."

Viggo slid from his chair and sidled up next to her. He was too close to be considered polite as he met her gaze beseechingly. "Don't be hasty. I wasn't prepared for a bride. I hadn't been expecting you. My home is not yet equipped for a woman. Tell me what it is that you need to make it a home and I will fetch it for you."

Fetch it from where? She wanted to demand. *I see no sign of wealth.* Was he a thief? One couldn't exactly stop a dragon from stealing their furniture if he took a liking to it.

"For one, you need curtains for that opening. I'll freeze to death if this is the only source of heat." Already Eleanor was beginning to tremble again as the sweat cooled on her skin. She sat up, wrapping her arms around herself.

He leaned in, mouth hovering very near hers. "I can keep you warm."

She smacked him lightly and scooted away. "Are you a philanderer? Will I find you've bedded half a hundred women and discarded them? I will not lie with a scoundrel, and I certainly will not be discarded by one again, *dragon.*"

"You are the only woman who has been in my bed," he purred.

"Yes, well, I wasn't in a bed when I had my virtue taken from me so that doesn't reassure me much."

"Not in a bed?"

Eleanor blushed and glanced at her hands. "It was a cleaning closet."

Viggo made a frightening noise and jumped from his place on the ground, rushing to the cave entrance and yanking off his clothing. She watched, half in shock and half in awe, as the muscles on his back rippled and stretched, opening to reveal the first hint of wings.

Moments later he was a dragon, coiled at the entrance with his head low to avoid hitting the ceiling.

"Where are you going?" She raced toward him, but it was too late. He leapt from the mouth of the cave, diving until he was nearly in the hot spring below before spreading his wings and pushing against the air. "What am I to do while you're gone?"

With a noise that could rival the dragon's growl, Eleanor stomped back over to where she'd begun moving furniture and wiping away dust. One day into her arrangement and she was already regretting her reckless journey north.

Were all dragons this irritating?

CHAPTER 5

ELEANOR

ELEANOR CLEANED UNTIL HER back ached. Even if Viggo wasn't proving to be a particularly good potential husband, she was relieved not to face Jerome and his demands of her. Besides, it was interesting. She was in a *dragon cave*. For many years Eleanor watched Viggo take to the skies, filling the evening with his trumpeting roar. More than once, she felt a tingle in her soles as he called out to the heavens, inexplicably drawn to the Winter Wilds each time he was about.

Grandmama claimed that was how dragons lured unwitting maidens to their demise. Their song summoned young women into the wilderness to be devoured once a year, when dragons needed virginal blood to maintain their power. Eleanor had her doubts now that she'd met a dragon.

With a weary sigh, she settled beside the fire and added another hunk of wood. Either Viggo didn't own an axe, or his lack of motivation extended to his woodchopping. The jagged edge was definitely the result of dragon claws crushing the wood. Looking at the pile that was quickly becoming woodchips and bark scraps, Eleanor wondered when Viggo would be back. The sun was already setting, and her hunger was nearly unbearable. Not to mention, she would quickly freeze without the fire now that she wasn't moving.

While cleaning the first quarter of the cave, Eleanor dug through the disorganized supplies in search of food scraps. There were sacks of flour, barrels of assorted grains, and two crates of apples that were too rotten for consumption. The rest was liquor and mead. Apparently Viggo spent a lot of time in his cups.

In a fit of anger, Eleanor chucked the crates of apples out of the cave entrance. One crashed down the side of the rock and landed in a mess at the base. The other splashed into the hot spring. She was sure she would regret it soon when the heat made the smell of rotten apples waft up the stone wall and into her shelter.

Twice she considered taking her things and leaving and twice she decided she would give it more time. For one, she wasn't sure she remembered how to make it back to the city. There was also the problem of getting down. Viggo was shaped like a man when he carried her up here, but he was much more agile than one. Eleanor was effectively trapped unless she wanted to risk breaking her neck.

The fire was dimming, and her shivering was becoming more insistent when she decided to climb under the furs for more warmth. Unfortunately, her first dress was still damp—and crunchy with frost—and the extra she wore was coated in spiderwebs and filth of all manner. Several minutes of rifling through a chest by the pallet found her a very large men's shirt that would have to replace her clothes until she could wash and dry both properly.

Eleanor gave it a cursory sniff. Wood smoke, cedar, and a scent she could only describe as *fire*, as if the smell somehow embodied his heat. Rushing so she didn't freeze, she quickly removed her dress and underthings and slipped into Viggo's shirt. Though it went nearly to her knees, it was much more exposing than a winter dress. She raced to the pallet and scurried as far under the furs as she could without suffocating.

Still no dragon. Perhaps he'd already grown bored with her and left her to rot. Grandmama warned her that most men were wandering scoundrels. Another of the many warnings Eleanor had not heeded.

She was sure that it was much too cold to fall asleep but somehow, she managed to drift off moments before a large shape swooped down from the clouds.

◦◇◦

V IGGO

Viggo contemplated leaving again. He brought her food and extra furs but neither would be enough to keep her warm through the coming storm. The woodpile was pathetically low, and he belatedly realized he hadn't been out to collect in nearly a week. Some mate he was.

If he'd known to expect her, perhaps he would have been a bit more prepared. But living alone in the wilds didn't require much effort for a dragon and Viggo had no desire for luxury. His home was a step down from poverty now that he was viewing it through Eleanor's eyes.

Sweet Eleanor, curled up snuggly in his bed, making shivering noises in her sleep. He ought to warm her. How could he when it was such a dangerous temptation? Viggo dropped his supplies by the fire and pulled back the furs, ready to hold her again as he had the night before. Only then did he realize she was clothed in his shirt. The sight of her pale legs covered by nothing but a short hem of fabric made his breath hitch.

Every inch of her was demanding to be kissed.

She'd been very clear on that point. Viggo had not earned a right to touch her as a lover. He was not welcome to take her to bed.

But at least he would do it *in* a bed! Gods, he almost shifted and left in another fit of fury. It was enough that a man other than him had touched his mate so intimately, but to do it in such a shameful place? No wonder she wanted away from whoever that bastard was. Eleanor clearly did not appreciate being treated as a dirty secret.

She would never be Viggo's secret. When she was finally his in heart and soul bond, he would sing his joy to all that could hear.

If only that time were now.

Gritting his teeth and praying for a strong will, Viggo once again pulled back the furs and slipped in behind Eleanor. Her reaction was instantaneous, turning toward the source of heat and squirming until she was pressed as closely to him as was possible. Her icy hands distracted him from the arousal throbbing between his legs. It wouldn't do for her to suffer like this because of him. She needed to be warm and comfortable here.

For the rest of the night, he focused on keeping his body temperature as warm as was needed to heat Eleanor in her sleep. It was easy to fall asleep in her arms.

———◆○◆———

ELEANOR

He was back, and he was constricted around her like a snake. Eleanor should have been more concerned that they were both half-dressed and embracing each other in his bed—yes, she had her arms around him too. But she reasoned it was innocent enough if it was the sole way for her to keep warm. Now what was she to do about dressing? It seemed too cold to even climb from bed, much less let the air touch her bare legs.

An angry growl reminded her that it had also been a full two days since she'd eaten more than winterberries. Quite a predicament she'd gotten herself in, wasn't it?

Her dismay only grew when she lifted her head to peer over Viggo's shoulder and saw violent white swirls where there should have been a sunrise.

A blizzard. Now even if she did convince him to carry her down from the cave, she would be stranded and frozen.

"Gods damn me and my recklessness," she cursed.

"But you wouldn't have the chance to woo a dragon for a husband if not for your recklessness."

"I'm questioning the wisdom of seeking to be a dragon bride," Eleanor responded, flopping her head back onto the pillow beside his.

Eyes like frozen lakes glimmered down at her, his pupils thin slits. Viggo quickly shuttered those eyes and gruffly asked, "Are you not pleased with your accommodations? Or is it the wifely duties?"

"I'm fine with wifely duties and a cave wouldn't be any worse than my previous home if you didn't treat it so poorly." Eleanor propped her hand on the bed and sat up. "Don't you care for the space you live in?"

He shrugged. "I'm a dragon. I can leave whenever I want and seek the skies."

"Well, I am not. I nearly fell to my death relieving myself yesterday!"

"I hadn't considered that."

"Neither of us has given this enough consideration. Perhaps I should go home. I've been far too impetuous lately."

A warm hand locked around her wrist and tugged her back down. "Do you always give up so easily?"

Eleanor scowled. "I'm not giving up."

"You are."

"Well, if I'm being perfectly honest—which I am far too often. Grandmama says it's a flaw and I should hold my tongue more—you have not made yourself a very desirable suitor. I don't mean to sound cruel, but I need to be practical and if I'm to look at my miserable life practically, I simply can't live in a cave with a dragon. I find you quite lovely to look at and the fact that you're a dragon intrigues me infinitely. I know I could stay awake half the night listening to you tell dragon stories—" She tapped the side of her head. "No, Eleanor. Practical.

"I am loath to wed a baker's son or a shepherd. I have been of age for two years and have not entertained any proposals of marriage. Being a dragon bride sounded rather thrilling in comparison to life in the capital and truly, I don't mind keeping a home but this, dearest dragon, is not a home. A woman cannot keep herself alive in a place like this. If I don't starve, I shall freeze to death." She rolled onto her back to move away from him. It was improper to be lying in his arms and she'd already spoiled herself enough. "As much as I hate it, I should have listened to my Grandmama's advice."

Suddenly a great weight came over her. Eleanor gasped when Viggo's hips aligned with hers and she felt *everything*. "I'm a dragon and you're a beautiful woman. What makes you think I'll simply let you go?"

Each word rolled off his tongue so seductively. She was caught between panic and desire. Warmth bloomed in places it never had when Jerome kissed her—certainly not when his hands fiddled with her underthings to make enough room for his entrance. Viggo had her pulse racing and her skin tingling strangely. Yet, she wasn't willing in whatever game he was playing, and it frightened her.

"Please, don't…" Was all she managed to mumble. It was the closest she'd come to admitting to Jerome she wasn't ready for what he sought either. Before that moment Eleanor hadn't realized how used she felt.

Viggo was gone as quick as he'd come, vanishing not just from on top of her but from the bed. "Never without your permission."

She raised a brow. "What if I never give my permission?"

"Then you can't possibly be a dragon bride." He shuffled around by the firepit, his movement difficult for her to see in the low light. "Enough of your fretting, El. I've provided you food, as a husband should. Now let me feed you while you make your wifely demands."

Eleanor wouldn't go as far as calling his behavior gentlemanly after that, but he wasn't climbing atop her either. There was no jest when he'd suggested he feed her. Viggo was doing just that, giving her one slow bite at a time. She might have complained if he hadn't reached into the cloth bag he must have returned with and offered not one, not two, but *three* winterberry pies. They weren't quite as good cold and when she told him so, he broke apart several of the mead crates and lit them on fire.

Unfortunately, he nearly lit the pie on fire too and they both decided cold was a fine way to eat it. Eleanor still hadn't stopped giggling at his complete lack of cooking competence.

"Have you never made a meal over a fire before?"

"I've never made a meal before." He told her, holding out the fork for her to take a bite. She hadn't asked where he'd gotten it and suspected it came from the pile of unknown junk. It tasted clean, so she didn't mind.

"Never? Not even a simple stew? A boiled egg?"

He smiled at her incredulity. "I didn't need to where I'm from."

"Because you're all dragons and just eat like animals?" She accepted the bite with a soft moan.

"Because the kitchen staff did it for us." So, he came from wealth. Why was he living in a cave now? Eleanor didn't imagine she would give up a life of luxury for this if she'd been born with it. So far, Viggo was decidedly vague with personal information, so she filed the tidbit away for later.

"Well, we haven't got that here and I can't eat a deer whole. We don't have to have a proper stove but if you want to keep a bride, you've got to have cooking equipment. How am I to make you supper without pots and pans? A rack to hang them over the fire?" She waved at the sloppy pit where splinters of crates burned. "That will not suffice for heat or cooking."

Viggo wore his signature smirk as she talked. The expression bordered on mocking, and she might have thought he was teasing her if he hadn't been nodding sincerely the whole time. He fed her another bite and asked, "What else?"

"Curtains." She pointed to the mouth of the cave. "The cold gets in far too easily. Look, there's snow on the floor!" Another mouthful of pie was forked her way. With the food still half chewed she added, "Rugs wouldn't hurt either—to warm the floors—but I know that's a bit frivolous."

"I can provide you with curtains and rugs."

She narrowed her eyes and watched him lick the fork after her last bite. "Where would you be providing them from? You aren't stealing, are you? I've no love for thieves and hustlers. My Grandmama and I have lost much to both."

A purring chuckle. "Trust me, I don't have a need to steal. I will come by everything honestly." He used his thumb to wipe sweet berry juice from the corner of her mouth and licked that too. Eleanor blushed as his tongue took a second taste. "More?"

"Yes," she breathed without comprehending the question. "More of what?"

"Food." His smirk became a wicked grin. "Unless there is something else you would like more of?"

"You've stuffed me with three pies, and you still have more food? Careful, you'll spoil me and then I'll be a terrible, fat wife."

"Perhaps I'm fattening you up to devour you." He drew out several soft cheeses and offered her a slice.

Eleanor's eyes widened. "Where did you get cheese? I've never had anything this fancy. We only eat what we can afford from Farmer Lockler's goats and it's always got an odd taste."

"I am more resourceful than I appear."

"So, you do have treasure. You've just hidden it." She tapped her temple. "Smart dragon. I hide my coin too. Otherwise, Grandmama will pilfer it and gamble it away."

"What kind of woman is your Grandmama?"

Her nose wrinkled as she quickly uttered, "Bitter." With a sigh she accepted another bite of cheese and stretched back onto the pillow. They'd yet to leave the bed, curled comfortably in the furs. "But she's been good to me, as good as she could be. She raised me when my mother and father would not. For that I owe her."

"I've always hated that sentiment. Family does not owe family for decency and care. It is the most basic requirement, the obligation of parenthood." Viggo finished off the cheese and swiped his fingers clean.

"She is not my parent, though, so how is she obligated?"

"She is the parent of your parent, thus she bears some responsibility for your existence."

Eleanor combed her fingers through her hair. It could use a good brushing, but she didn't want to leave the warmth of the furs to retrieve her brush. "I've never thought of it like that. Grandmama made me work to repay the effort she took as my caretaker."

"Ridiculous and petty. Your children do not owe you a price for requiring your care. Children are inherently in need of care and if you bring them into the world, *you* owe *them* at least that much." He almost sounded angry. Clearly this was an issue he'd thought about for a long time.

"Do you have many grievances with your family?"

"I'd rather not speak of my family." Eleanor decided to take that as a "yes."

"What would you like to speak about then? Will you tell me what it's like living in the Winter Wilds?"

Viggo eagerly obliged her, answering any and all questions that did not relate to his family or his origin. There seemed to be no limits to what he was willing to talk about and more than once his audacity had Eleanor blushing. It wasn't only words that had her blushing. They burned as many crates as they had but eventually the fire was not enough to keep her warm. She wiggled into a pair of his pants and the wool was soothing, but it still wasn't adequate to defeat the harsh winds ripping into the mouth of the cave.

With Viggo as the only true source of heat, she found herself seated in his lap, his arms secured tightly around her. He wasn't shy about the heavy weight between his legs or how it twitched when she readjusted herself on his thighs. So long as he didn't act on it without her permission, she decided to be flattered. Mary would mock her for that, claiming that men could be aroused by a horse if it was comely enough, but Eleanor didn't think that true of Viggo.

They passed most of the day in bed. Eleanor only left the safety of its warmth twice to relieve herself and that was awkward and mortifying. Viggo told her stories of watching wolf packs from above as they chased an injured elk. He talked of bear cubs in trees and moose bugling to each other over the wetlands. From above he'd seen the world moving the way it usually would without audience, the natural order in motion undisturbed by man.

"Are the animals not frightened of you?"

"The ones that serve as breakfast have a healthy fear when I'm on the prowl, but even they stand and graze when I'm only passing overhead. They've come to know me as just another inhabitant of the wilds." His voice was a deep vibration beneath her, lulling her into a drowsy state as she rested her head on his chest. It was terribly intimate and in ordinary circumstances Eleanor would have been uncertain about allowing such closeness. But alone in the Winter Wilds with a storm raging around them, she was pleased to find shelter in his arms.

This, she thought, was what a marriage should feel like. Not two people securing their future by providing skill sets to compensate each other for their labor and certainly not a woman trading her womb for food on the table. A good marriage should be as a good house—stable, safe, the place you long for when the day is harrowing. She never would have anticipated that such things could come from a dragon of all places.

Stranger things had happened, she was sure.

Eventually the purr of his words and the warmth of his embrace became a sleep tonic for her overworked body. As her aches vanished, her eyes drooped further and further until she saw nothing but black.

The last she heard of him was a murmur beside her ear. "Sleep, sweet El. I'll keep you warm."

CHAPTER 6

T̲HE STORM DIDN'T PASS for two days, so for two days Eleanor and Viggo huddled on his pallet. He fed her cold pies, cheese, and salted meat while telling stories of the great Winter Wilds. It was odd to be curled up in the arms of a complete stranger, but Eleanor quickly lost her insecurities. Viggo was clearly not uninterested, yet he was honorable for the entirety of the storm.

Did that mean he wasn't flirting mercilessly and hinting at what he wanted from her should she pass his test? Of course not. The man couldn't say two words that didn't inspire thoughts of sweat slicked skin and clashing lips.

A nice change of pace, really. Jerome never bothered to woo her beyond one or two shallow compliments. In fact, Eleanor couldn't remember why she was so besotted with him now that she'd gotten away. Was it his princely looks? The cleanness of his hands, so unblemished by toil? Or perhaps it was his vocabulary. He did use a lot of big words.

As mortifying as it was to admit to herself, Eleanor was beginning to fear her desire for him had been equally shallow. He was a handsome prince that deigned speak to a lowly maid. His attention made her feel seen and so she basked in it. What a fool she was. Jerome must have seen it too. Clearly Eleanor wasn't the first maid he'd dragged into a cleaning closet to satisfy his masculine urges. It was too practiced to be a one-time event.

And to think she'd almost felt guilty for taking that connection from his bride to be.

Frustration with herself served no good. Eleanor decided to cleanse her mind by finally extricating herself from the bed and getting back to work in the cave that could be her home. As soon as the snow died down and the winds lost their violent edge, Viggo left to collect firewood. Though it wasn't cut in uniform pieces as she was accustomed to, she was grateful for the massive pile stacked by the pit.

Still wearing Viggo's clothes—served him right if they got dust on them—Eleanor tackled the pile of abused items in the corner. There were misused iron pans that were hopelessly rusted, various broken plates and bowls, the leg of a chair that she couldn't match with any of the current furniture, and crates of spoiled food. Those were sorted into a new pile. None of that rubbish needed to stay here any longer, and she intended to ask Viggo to remove it as soon as he returned.

Not everything had been deemed useless. There were crumpled books that only need their pages straightened and a shelf to sit tidily on. Three lovely wool shirts were tangled together. Eleanor saw nothing wrong with them except a few tears that needed mending. She set one aside for herself, intent to use it to make herself another dress since the fabric was so warm. There was also a crate of ceramic plates that were only chipped.

Her favorite find by far was a small wooden box full of cooking spices. Why it had been tossed with the rest of the waste, she didn't know. There were several spices she recognized by smell—she couldn't read the labels—and several she'd never used before. Each had a delightful aroma that made her stomach rumble.

The box too was a work of art. Shined mahogany with a gilded trim that shone in the firelight. The most spectacular part, however, was the crest carved into the wood. Two dragons locked together in an elegant dance around a sword. Whether they were truly dancing or battling, she couldn't say. A faint familiarity sparked when she stared at the carving, but she couldn't place where she'd seen that particular crest before.

"So lovely," she whispered, running her finger along the gold trim and setting it carefully on the bed. Eleanor had dusted items of such beauty when she worked in the castle, but she'd never had the opportunity to hold one reverently in her palms.

Viggo returned moments later, landing with the skitter of claws on stone. A thump drew her attention to him, and she looked down to see a marvelous sight.

"A whole buck? Where on earth did you find such a prize?" A stupid question, she realized. He was a dragon. An elk was as easily plucked from the ground as a flower to him.

Viggo shifted his serpentine neck in her direction, crystalline eyes studying her. Without warning he darted forward, his scales sliding across the stone. Eleanor backed up a step, freezing before she accidentally put her foot into the fire pit.

She wasn't frightened, not quite, but she had a feeling Viggo was enjoying stalking her. A strange shiver took her, and she had to steel herself when his large head came to rest inches from her.

Hot gusts of breath blew her braid across her shoulder. Eleanor squealed when his mouth opened wide, revealing the pointed teeth responsible for the elk's end. A long, pink tongue slipped from between those teeth, wetting her neck and face before retreating.

Eleanor stood speechless as Viggo shrunk down from dragon to man. He faced her unashamedly in his naked state, not bothering to hide his significant arousal. It was impossible not to stare at his cock. The thing was much bigger than she imagined. Though, Mary had once told her they vary in size. A lot, apparently.

"Do you like what you see, El?"

"Yes." She clapped her hand over her mouth. "I meant to say, 'please put some clothes on.'"

"But you're enjoying my nudity."

Admittedly, she was. Viggo was an even greater work of art than the box of spices. Lean muscle covered every inch of him, flexing with his breath. His pale skin was completely unblemished but for the dark blonde hair that dotted his chest and trailed from his stomach down to his manhood. The braids in his hair were undone, and it flowed over his shoulder and around his chest in pale cascades. He looked like he was born in the Winter Wilds, made of the same stuff as the bonewood trees.

Yes, Eleanor was very much enjoying his nudity. She was finding it nearly impossible not to cross over to him and touch him. Though she was no longer innocent, she hadn't gained any true experience. What did those ridges of muscle feel like on a man's stomach? How would his cock respond if she touched it? Was it as hot as the rest of him? Would it burn her tongue if she tasted it?

"*Eleanor*." That single, guttural word made her legs feel as though they were becoming liquid. Heat was gathering in her chest, dripping languidly down to the space between her legs.

She looked up sharply to his eyes, suddenly mortified. Surely, he couldn't tell what she was thinking. Could dragons read minds? They were fabled to have all manner of powers. Eleanor hadn't thought to ask.

Pivoting, she covered the half of her face that could still view him in her peripherals and fished for a pair of pants out of his trunk, tossing them feebly as her hands shook.

"What are you going to do with that elk?" She was desperate to change the topic from her perverse thoughts of him. It worked—mostly. Though it would take hours to process, the elk reminded her that she was once again starving. At least working in the castle, she was fed a meal once a day.

"You're going to butcher it and preserve it so that we don't go hungry all winter long."

Eleanor whirled, not caring if he was naked still or not. "Preserve this entire elk? Did you bring salt too? A barrel for mixing brine? Where are your butchering knives?" He didn't expect her to preserve an entire elk with the mismatched cutlery from his junk pile, did he?

Viggo scratched his chin, glaring at the dead creature on the floor. "Is it so complicated to save meat?"

"Have you never preserved food for winter before?"

"Of course not." He seemed to think better of his pompous response. "A dragon can eat when he wants. There is no need to cut or cook meat."

"Right." Eleanor covered her face, willing patience. *Lazy dragon.* "I'm going to need supplies. Tools, too."

"I didn't realize a wife could be so demanding." It was a tease, but she was hungry and not in the mood for teasing.

"I'm asking so very little of you compared to an ordinary man, *dragon*. I want only for a humble kitchen to cook and the food to fill it. Is that asking so much?" She tossed her hands up. "No wonder wives are always henpecking! How could they not when men are so clueless about matters of the home?"

"I'm inexperienced," he said defensively. "I will learn if you teach me." At least he was willing.

"Very well. We will cook what we can of this tonight, but it will spoil without the proper amount of salt." Eleanor flitted back and forth, hoping for any kind of sharp utensil. "If only I could butcher it."

Viggo took the back leg of the animal and heaved. There was a wet crunch moments before he was handing her a mangled haunch. "For you, sweet El."

"What a charming gift." She laughed despite herself, taking the heavy piece of meat and carrying it to the makeshift kitchen she'd created by the fire. It was just a clean slab of rock where she could drag charcoal for heating food, but it was much better than having nothing. "If I could just get the skin off, we can roast it on the spit. I'm eager to try some of your spices with it."

"Spices?" Eleanor pointed to the lovely box. The purring tone left Viggo's voice, and his next words were uttered with a cold edge. "Where did you get that?"

She swallowed, hoping she hadn't crossed a boundary she was unaware of. "It was in that pile of discarded items, under a bunch of books and clothes."

Without warning Viggo snatched the box and tossed it across the cave. He threw it violently enough that the box splintered on impact, loose spices flying everywhere.

"No!" Eleanor jumped from the fire, running to the sad remains. With one hand she made a tray. The other uselessly tried to scoop some of the bigger lumps of spices from the floor. That much spice was worth a fortune. Most herbs grew poorly in Brula and were imported from Gazar and the other southern islands. She could have spent a year's pay and not collected as big a supply. "Why did you do that?"

"Leave it!" He boomed. "I never want to see you wearing that crest."

"I wasn't *wearing* it. What on earth has gotten into you?" Her voice trembled, as did her hands. A violent man was a bad enough husband. A violent dragon was a death sentence.

"Do not touch those spices!" He growled, lunging for her and swatting her hand away.

Startled, Eleanor stumbled back, falling painfully onto her rear. Viggo's eyes widened, and he backed away. In one blink he went from man to dragon, his reptilian head smacking against the narrow ceiling where she knelt. He continued backing up, snatching the elk in his maw and dropping from the cave entrance.

She stared open-mouthed for several minutes. Only when she rose from the ground, dusting herself off, did she realize there were tears wetting her cheeks. How unfair that wealthy men—even if they were dragons—could destroy whatever they pleased with no consequence. Jerome destroyed women and Viggo destroyed priceless goods. For what purpose? Why did *spices* anger him so?

Not spices, she thought. It was that crest. Setting by the fire and tossing on another log, Eleanor closed her eyes and tried to picture it again. One of the many wealthy lords that served in the king's court flew that flag, but if she'd seen it, she couldn't remember it clearly.

It was a hint of Viggo's mysterious origin. Had someone from that lineage wronged him? Obviously, he was highborn, if dragon-men—*drakonmein*—could be. Or at the very least, he came from a life of privilege. His mannerisms and the way he spoke were too like the courtiers she served at the castle to be a coincidence. Were there Brulian lords that were secretly dragons?

There were rumors of multiple dragons to the east. Viggo could have belonged to them and cut ties.

But why?

And why did he have to destroy the spices? Gods, she was never going to recover from the grief of losing those precious satchels.

With no more enthusiasm for this game of playing dragon bride, Eleanor got to work on the tedious job of stripping the elk haunch. Hours seemed to pass before it was finally coming off the spit, sizzling and smelling as good as unsalted, unseasoned meat could.

She chewed the gamey meal dispassionately, wiping greasy fingers on Viggo's shirt when she was finished. Afterward she tossed two more broken chunks of wood into the fire pit and crawled under the furs.

Tomorrow, she would ask him to carry her down the cliff so she could journey home.

CHAPTER 7

VIGGO

LIVING IN ISOLATION HAD made him volatile, Viggo was real-ized. It was true that he'd always had a temper and that even thinking of his family made it flare out of control. But when he saw the look on Eleanor's face after he smashed the gift—the *bribe*—that his parents offered him the last time they spoke, he knew he'd gone too far.

Maybe his entire scheme had gone too far. Why did he have to be so superior?

Because he was angry that she'd given herself to another. Why should he woo her? Didn't he deserve to be wooed after she'd com-mitted such a crime against their future bond? But she didn't know about mates or that he'd been looking for his for so many miserable years.

Perhaps honesty would have served his cause better.

Eleanor waited for him by the fire when he returned the next after-noon. She was draped in one of the furs from the pallet, clearly cold and hungry. Gods, he was a villain. He'd all but imprisoned her and left her with nothing to sustain herself when he was off chasing his darker moods.

"I've brought you a gift." Several, as he should have from the start. A mate was not obligated to stay—especially without a bond—and he could see by her face that she was ready to be rid of him.

What a mess.

"You can't make me forget your bad behavior with gifts. You, dragon, are erratic and spoiled. And your violence scares me."

Viggo dropped the large hemp bag he used to bring goods to and from the cave, quickly dressing so he could take a knee before her. "You must forgive me, El. I've been alone for a very long time, and it seems I don't know how to behave around a woman."

"Or how to behave at all. Your home is a pigsty."

"Ah, yes. Yes, it is. I've had no need to clean it."

"I think it best I return home. This endeavor was a foolish one."

"No!" He said much too vehemently. "You were right. I should make myself a desirable match for you too. In less than a week you've made my home feel as a home should. Let me do the rest."

Her chestnut eyes narrowed at him. "Why should you? I came to you making demands with no inviting prospects. I was hoping you would eat me."

"Oh, I'll eat you." He licked his lips suggestively.

Eleanor smacked his hand from her knee and scowled. "Are all dragons so lecherous or is it just you?"

"Come see my gifts." He changed the topic, motioning for her to join him closer to the fire.

"Gifts? I thought it was only one."

"I got carried away."

"Carried away where?"

"It doesn't matter." He held open the sack.

Eleanor reached inside, her eyes fixed on him the whole time. Gods, she was resplendent, even wrapped in wrinkled furs with her hair in a simple braid. If lavish gifts were what she required for happiness, he would shower her with them daily. No expense would be spared if it meant he spent each day basking in her beauty.

"Why are you staring at me so fiercely? Is this a trick?"

"I've searched for you endlessly," he admitted in a hoarse whisper.

"Searched for me? What do you—oh!" She pulled the heavy wooden box from his bag. "More spices?"

"To replace what I ruined. I am sorry for my temper."

Her eyes became saucers. "How? How did you come by these?" Suspicion replaced surprise. "Are you secretly wealthy?"

It wasn't a secret to anyone that knew his family name. To her, he must look like a beggar, living in a cave with few furnishings and fewer possessions. "It's not a secret. You never inquired about my wealth."

"They smell lovely." She held the chest to her nose and inhaled deeply, humming a satisfied noise. With a soft click she shut the box again, running her fingers over the plain wood. "The box isn't as lovely, but I suppose that's a frivolous concern."

Guilt made a second lap around his mind. "There's more."

Startled by his voice, she set the spices aside and dug through the bag. A cloak made of wolf pelts as white as snow came out next. It was a one-of-a-kind piece, or so the shopkeeper told him. Next came several pots and pans. They were small but adequate for his unique fireplace. Finally came a leather belt with six sheathed knives.

"They're for butchering, but you can also use this thick one for vegetables." He tapped the knife on the end of the row.

Eleanor held the belt carefully between her fingers, staring a bit too intently at it. Her eyes glazed with tears, one of them spilling quickly down her cheek and dripping onto the leather.

"Sweetest El." He cupped her face, brushing away the wet trail the tear left and catching several more with his fingers. "What have I done to make you weep?"

"These are..." She sniffled. "They're too nice. I don't think I'm deserving of such nice things."

"Of course, you are. If you're to be my wife, you'll have only the finest things."

"I'm just a maid." She turned her face from his hand. "A silly, poor maid without even virtue to offer. I don't know why you would give these to me."

"To make you happy." He scooted closer, taking her hands and bringing them to his lips. "But it seems I have done the opposite."

"No, you haven't. I'm grateful. Truly, I am so grateful."

"Then look at me."

Reluctantly, she lifted her gaze. "It's hard to look at you. I'm so embarrassed. You must think me such a dolt."

"I think you're stunning."

"You flatter me." She clearly didn't believe him. With a delicate finger she traced the sheath of one of the knives. "I've never had something so special." Quieter, she admitted, "No one has ever given me a gift before."

Viggo realized then that he hadn't bothered getting to know her at all. She listened with rapt attention as he talked of himself. What had he asked about her? He knew nothing of her childhood, the home she came from, the life she led before him. In his mind all that mattered was that she was his mate, a possession more than a person. Eleanor was right to turn his advances down. How was he any better than the man that spurned her and sent her running into the Winter Wilds?

"Will you tell me about yourself? After you're fed, of course. I can hear your stomach." He dug through the bottom of the bag and fished out the bacon and bread he'd purchased, not knowing exactly what she would eat besides pie and cheese.

"Thank you," she whispered. "Thank you for the gifts."

Sweetest El, I will give you everything your heart desires.

"I'm sorry for calling you spoiled."

"You weren't wrong."

"Well, if I'm to be your wife, don't expect me to spoil you." She wiped beneath her eyes with her knuckles. "Shall I make us supper?"

"I thought you weren't going to spoil me."

"Tonight, I'll make exception since you brought me such wonderful gifts."

S HE MADE EXCEPTIONS EVERY night, cooking him a myriad of pies and stews with the ingredients he brought her. What was once a horrid chore—returning to a nearby city to search the market for goods—had become one of his favorite parts of the day. He enjoyed surprising Eleanor with new and luxurious foods as much as he enjoyed the meals she prepared with them. After eight days she had significant rations in case of another winter storm—they were frequent around the solstice—or to sate her hunger when he was out hunting.

Each night they twined their arms around each other, lounging by the fire and talking far too late into the night. She told him of her childhood—the chores, her grandmama's gambling, the strange ways she found to make a copper here and there—and of the dreams she had of building a true family for herself one day.

Viggo found himself less preoccupied with the bond. What they were sharing now was as vital as that magical connection. He had to learn her before they could become one. And Eleanor fascinated him as much as he fascinated her. Though she couldn't read, she knew about so many topics. Apparently, hours spent bargaining for trade with Brulian locals and sailors in the port gained her knowledge as well as resources.

"There is not."

"There is so! Six sailors claimed to have seen it." She sat up, contorting her hand to mimic the creature she spoke of. "It had twenty tentacles as thick as tree trunks. They climbed from the water and wrapped so tightly 'round a ship that it splintered."

"How did the sailors live to tell the tale then?"

"Easy." She rested her head back on his chest. "They were rescued by plump seals and carried to shore."

Viggo snorted with laughter. "You've made this all up."

"I have not! I heard the story straight from the sailors' mouths. They were white as sheets when they told it."

"Perhaps they'd spent too long at sea."

"Perhaps you're too skeptical."

He pinched her side. "If I'm skeptical, you're *gullible*. Are these the same sailors that told you of singing fish ladies?"

"*Mermaids*." She huffed indignantly. "And yes, they were. That doesn't mean it isn't true. Sailors see so many strange, faraway places."

"Somehow, I doubt there are that many strange and faraway places between here and Gazar."

"You wouldn't know."

"I could find out. I'll simply fly over the ocean. Much easier than sailing, and safer too."

Eleanor quieted, absently dancing her fingertip between his pecks. Viggo tried to ignore how quickly such a simple touch ignited his desire for her. Though he *was* enjoying these nights of talking, he couldn't completely ignore the instinct to claim her rightly.

"The Winter Solstice is coming," she murmured after a time.

"Yes, in three days."

"Do dragons celebrate the solstice?"

"Of course." He combed his fingers through her hair. "I'm Brulian as much as you are. And except for the occasional journey through the sky, I'm as much a man as any other."

"I'll have to disagree with that last bit." She chuckled at a joke that she shared only with herself. "How do you celebrate way out here?"

Viggo shrugged. "I light the ceremonial candles." Since leaving his family home and coming to live in the Winter Wilds, he hadn't celebrated the old holidays with enthusiasm. They were meant to be shared events.

"That's all? No spiced wine? No singing? No watching the winter lights?"

"I see them from time to time through the cave entrance."

"Isn't it lonely to celebrate that way?"

"I suppose it's a little quieter than I'm accustomed to."

Eleanor sat up again, her eyes sparkling. "Can we go somewhere to celebrate? You go to market so you can clearly walk the streets without care. Why not leave the wilds and spend some time in the city?"

"I don't visit the capital when I go to market." He shuttered his expression, hoping to hide his revulsion for that cesspit of corruption the courtiers called home. "I go further north, to Vannar."

"Why go so far? Brula is only—"

"I will not go to Brula, Eleanor. Do not ask that of me."

She slumped back into bed, this time resting her head on her own pillow. "Never mind. It was a silly request."

Gods damn him. "No, it wasn't silly, El." He smoothed his thumb over her freckled cheek. "Would it make you happy to celebrate the solstice in a city?"

"So very happy."

"Then we shall go to Vannar to celebrate together." Viggo stilled his hand. "Though, it's much too far to walk. We will have to fly."

That signature brightness flashed back into her eyes. "You're going to take me flying?"

He couldn't help but laugh. "Does everything make you this excited?"

"*Everything*," she agreed.

CHAPTER 8

ELEANOR WAS ALREADY IN love with the Winter Solstice holiday before Viggo took her to celebrate. There was delicious food, gifts exchanged with friends and neighbors, joyful music from dusk onward, and, best of all, lights. So many lights twinkling prettily in orb shaped lanterns. Some families saved candles all year to decorate their homes on solstice night. It would be long and cold, but the people of Brula would not live in shadows.

Those beautiful dancing lights were a whole different work of art from above. Though the wind ripped at her fine fur cloak and the frosty air stung her eyes, Eleanor didn't huddle into Viggo's scaly arm. He clutched her tightly to his chest, carefully cradling her as he navigated the skies.

"I love flying!" She shouted to him over the rush of wings.

He made a rumbling noise like laughter before tucking into himself and descending to the forest on the outskirts of Vannar. She'd never been to a city outside of the capital and was surprised to see such a thriving place this far up the coast.

"They make their wealth selling imported spices and other fine goods. In the summer you can find strange fruits shipped all the way from Gazar," Viggo explained to her this morning.

Even by dragon it was a further journey than the capital. She hadn't gleaned precisely why he avoided Brula so thoroughly, but she didn't care to dig into that conversation tonight.

Tonight, was all about celebrating the light in the darkest times, the joy that winter was halfway from its end.

"Your clothes." She blushed as she handed him the sack he usually traveled with. Viggo transformed the instant they hit the ground, leaving her to avert her eyes or get quite a view. It was too dark to see much. That didn't mean she hadn't peeked.

"Are you nervous to be here?"

"No," she said too tersely. "I'm nervous for you to see your solstice gift. I have no coin to buy you something and I couldn't exactly walk to market to trade winterberries..." Eleanor fiddled with her cloak. "I'm making excuses. I'll be thrilled if you like it. I'll understand if you find it too simple for someone with such refined breeding."

Viggo snorted. "Don't call me refined. Where's my gift? Is it in here?" He grinned, digging through the sack and donning the pants she neatly folded for him. Next came one of the lovely silk shirts she'd found among his things.

Eleanor wanted to look away when he noticed the new stitching on the right breast of the shirt, but she was frozen to the spot, staring at his face for signs of disappointment. She caught herself doing that often, waiting for some sign that she'd finally worn out her welcome and that he would send her away.

Viggo ran a finger gently over the blue dragon threaded into the fabric. She'd been careful not to make it look like the crest from the spice chest, instead mimicking his form as best she could. The wings were difficult to get right, and she'd been rushed to finish before the holiday arrived, but the end result made her proud. Of all the skills she possessed, sewing was one of the few she was truly good at.

"You did this yourself?"

She swallowed. "I did."

"You're very talented." He pulled the shirt over his head, running a palm down the breast to feel the thread work again. "A lovely gift from a lovely bride."

"Do you mean it?"

He took her hand and brought it to his lips, warming her instantly. "Of course. You didn't have to get me a gift, but I love what you've done."

"You've given me so many gifts." Eleanor followed as he led her to the open gates and under an archway decorated with white winter-berry flowers and holly.

"I needed to show you that I would make a suitable husband for you."

"Well, I wasn't expecting expensive spices from across the world. I only meant you couldn't leave me to starve in a cave while you were out bird watching." She tilted her chin to admire the dozens of solstice lanterns above them.

Viggo escorted her from one street to another. They listened to a choir sing traditional melodies that welcomed the stars on this long night. Vendors offered them pies and sweet, hot milk drinks and they eagerly indulged. A spiced venison sausage was shared between them. Eleanor had never felt so full before in her life.

Though Vannar appeared small on the outside, it housed as many wonderful sights and secrets as Brula. The port was not only meant for sailors arriving with goods from across the continent. There were funny shaped boats with even funnier names where raucous parties were held.

"House boats?" Eleanor frowned when Viggo explained. "Isn't that an oxymoron? How can a house be a boat?"

"The insides are decorated lavishly. Wealthy families live in them during the summer months, spending days at sea just to enjoy the sunshine and the breeze."

"Seems frivolous if you ask me." She puffed a steamy breath. "How do you know so much about these house boats?"

"I've spent my fair share of time on them." He answered, steering her out of the way of several drunken revelers. "My brother and I indulged a bit too much in our youth."

A woman squealed, drawing their attention just as she stood on the deck of one of the larger boats and lifted her skirt for passersby to see what was beneath. She wore no stockings or underthings, despite the cold.

"Indulged in what, exactly?" Eleanor turned sharply down another street, giving him her back.

Viggo chuckled as he caught up, taking her hand and placing it in the crook of his elbow. She allowed him to, but only because she forgot her gloves and her hands were cold. "Only in drink. Are you jealous, El?"

"Well, if I'm to be your bride, I have a right, don't I?"

"I too should be jealous then. Tell me of your previous lover so I can kill him."

She yanked her hand away and crossed her arms, her boots clicking loudly as she hurried down another street. "No. You look far too serious about that killing part."

"Perhaps I am serious."

"Does that mean you *are* jealous?"

"Of course." He caught up with her, placing a firm hand on her shoulder so she couldn't speed away again. "He laid hands on what belongs to me."

"I'm not your wife yet."

Viggo pulled her to a stop. They'd followed the maze of roads to the town square. A massive fir stood proudly in the center of the square, its magnificent branches decorated with shiny silver bobbles and tiny glowing lanterns of similar design. At its very peak there was a golden star with a flickering candle inside. Eleanor couldn't fathom how they got it up there.

All around them strings of lanterns hung from buildings and light poles. Interwoven into those strings were bundles of dried love crocus—the kissing flower.

"I would like you to be," he said quietly behind her.

Eleanor held her breath as she glanced over her shoulder at him. His eyes had shifted to that ghostly blue, his pupil a fine line. "Truly?"

Viggo came around her, cupping his free hand as if he was holding something fragile. "Truly."

The metal he slipped around her marriage finger was warm from his palm. He kept it covered, smirking as the desire to look made her squirm.

"I've proved a good wife to you, despite my shortcomings?" For some reason she feared this was a cruel jape.

"You have no shortcomings." He tucked a loose hair behind her ear. "And I don't care if you keep my house or wreck it. I find I am fascinated by the way you blurt things without thinking and how brazenly you live each moment. What kind of woman marches into the Winter Wilds to ask a dragon to marry her? That is the type of absurdity I've fallen in love with."

"In love with?" But she hadn't even kissed him, as Jerome claimed she would have to for him to know how he felt. She'd given him nothing of her but her company.

"Yes, El. I do believe you've made me fall helplessly in love with you." He revealed the ring on her hand. A sapphire gleamed up at her from a band of silver.

"Viggo, this is too—"

"Shh. It matches your beauty. Now look up."

She did. They were standing directly below a cluster of kissing flowers. Eleanor did what she'd wanted to do for many, many days then. She kissed him. It wasn't quite as gentle a kiss as she meant. Viggo was rather tall and there was some jumping required to reach him. He handled her clumsiness with grace, wrapping his arms around her waist when she tumbled into him and lifting her from the ground.

"I would like to be your wife," she whispered against his lips.

He smiled even as he kissed her again. And again, and again until a man with two children by his side cleared his throat and reminded them where they were.

"We should go home," Eleanor said urgently.

"Yes, I'm inclined to agree," he growled, taking her hand and leading her back through the streets and to the city gates, her cloak billowing behind her in their haste.

⸻◆⸻

V IGGO

Eleanor didn't stop shivering when he lit a fire and placed her next to it. Even after wrapping a second fur around her, she still shook more than Viggo was comfortable with. Flying with her during the winter months was not a wise idea. He didn't intend to repeat his mistake.

"I wanted to k-kiss you again," she chattered, "But my lips are so c-cold."

"I shouldn't have taken you." Viggo came to sit next to her, unfastening her cloak and hanging it over a chair.

"Yes! You sh-should have. This was the b-best solstice I've ever c-celebrated." She wrapped her arms around his neck when he scooped her up, not hesitating to let him carry her to the bed.

He pulled back the furs and gently rested Eleanor on the fluffy cot he made his bed from. She wiggled over so there was plenty of room for him to join her. With his long limbs and broad chest, the pallet bed was scarcely big enough for the both of them without Eleanor sprawling atop him. Most nights she'd taken to doing just that, basking in his body heat while she slept. It was a wonder he'd gone as long as he did without kissing her.

Now that he had a taste, he was never going to be able to stop.

"Better?" He whispered into her hair when she finally stopped shaking.

"Very much. Are all dragons this warm?"

"Don't concern yourself with other dragons. I'm the only one that will ever warm you."

She snorted. "Are all dragons this self-assured?"

"Generally speaking, yes. It's in our nature to be egotistical."

Eleanor laughed softly, her breath tickling his neck. With a sigh she lifted her head until their eyes met, lips only inches apart. "I'm going to kiss you again."

Though he was tempted, he didn't beg her. Instead Viggo took a handful of her hair and tilted her head back, guiding her exactly where he wanted until their lips collided. Without an audience and the brisk winter night there was no fettering the rush of want. She was his mate, and she'd been in his bed for weeks without him making a single attempt to seduce her out of her clothes. All that pent up desire was fighting to be sated.

His tongue slipped between her lips, taking in a better taste of her. Eleanor made a startled noise, and he inhaled it, pleased he caught her by surprise. There was so much more he could do to her that would have her gasping.

When they were both breathless, he moved from her lips, using his hold in her hair to present her neck to him. First Viggo kissed down to her collar bone. Then he travelled back up the way he'd come with his tongue. He was nipping at her pulse point when she squirmed and made a frustrated noise.

"What troubles you, sweet El?"

Her cheeks were flushed, and she seemed sheepish when she asked, "When will we marry?"

She was worrying about that now? Truth be told he hadn't given it much thought. It was hardly important to his kind once the bond was made, except for appearances in civilized society. "Soon. As soon as you want."

"And if we don't..." She chewed her lip, drawing his attention to how rosy and swollen it was. "Well, if we know we're going to get married, there's no harm if we don't wait, right?"

He tensed, his blood pumping so furiously that he was painfully hard. "Wait for what?"

"You know."

"I don't, El. Tell me what you're asking of me." Her cheeks became an even pinker shade. "Let me hear you say it," he purred.

"I want you," she breathed, pulling at the laces on the side of her dress and loosening them so that the fabric slipped down her shoulders. "I want to take you into me."

"El." Viggo knew his eyes were glowing, could see the light on her face in the dim cave. "There is no going back if I take you. No matter what, you will belong to me."

"You will never leave me?"

"I couldn't bear to."

Eleanor pulled the top of her dress down further, revealing the rounds of her breasts. "Then I think we've waited long enough."

Viggo made quick work of their clothing, tossing all of it in a heap on the floor. Goosebumps dotted Eleanor's skin as the cold air swooped in to take advantage of her nakedness. He remedied her temperature by covering her with his body, pressing against her as their mouths mirrored what their bodies would soon do.

At first, she moved in rhythm with him, but as his hips lowered, grinding against her, Eleanor began to tense. Her shoulders were rigid, and her legs were locked in place around him.

Viggo lifted his head. "Have you changed your mind?"

"No, I haven't." She scowled.

"Why are you so tense?"

Her answer was quiet and shy. "Sorry, I was only readying myself."

"Readying yourself?"

"For the discomfort."

Discomfort? Why would she want this if she anticipated pain? "I don't know what your expectations are, dear El, but I promise that you will feel no discomfort. This is meant to be enjoyable for the both of us."

"Is it truly?" The sincerity of her question almost angered him. What a poisonous world Brula was for women. The courts taught them to be ashamed of all their base desires, all their instincts, then expected them to serve those exact instincts in their men.

Viggo would show her a better world. "Truly."

He slid to the side of her, propping his body up on his elbow so he could lean over her chest. Eleanor gasped as his mouth came over her right breast, sucking her nipple into his mouth and dancing his tongue along it. With his free hand he took her other nipple, pinching lightly and giving her the thrill of almost-pain.

Viggo enjoyed that same thrill as Eleanor's hands slipped into his hair, gripping at the back of his head and pulling. He let her guide him by that built in rein, pressing his mouth harder onto her nipple. Experimentally he sank his teeth into her flesh, nipping and sucking until he was sure she would have purple marks all over her breast.

"Oh," she breathed. "That is...provocative."

He hummed along her skin, skimming his lips down to her belly button. "What does it provoke, El?"

"Desire."

"Where do you desire me?"

She took his hand, dragging it down her stomach and over her mound. For someone who had been prepared to make love simply for his pleasure, she was certainly well acquainted with her own cravings. She pressed two of his fingers into the peak of her core and he took it from there, circling that aroused flesh ever so softly. When her breathing picked up too much, he stopped, moving down to feel the growing wetness on her lips.

After a few short minutes of torment, Eleanor was desperate. She bucked her hips at his hands, following them each time they retreated with a panting whine. "Please, Viggo. You promised pleasure. This is torture."

"Oh? This doesn't please you at all?" He finally pressed into her with more pressure, and she gasped.

"It...pleases...me."

He rose, spreading her legs wide and letting his cock drop to meet her wet lips. "Would this please you?"

"Yes. Gods, yes!"

Still circling her with one finger, Viggo slipped inside her. Despite how wet and ready she was, Eleanor felt tight around him. That tightness only increased when he was fully seated within her, and her body rocked with orgasm. He almost finished right then, too overcome with the way she screamed his name. How could such a desperate, feral sound be so heavenly? He felt as if this was a moment of worship.

"Viggo, please."

"Please?" Viggo lowered his body until their chests met, bringing his lips inches from hers. "Whatever are you begging for? Haven't I given you what you wanted?"

"Yes, and now you've spoiled me." She caught his bottom lip, biting down just hard enough to draw him closer. "I want more."

"Then you shall have more." With a groan he withdrew, then thrust into her.

His hips were fervent, his body aching for release. But Viggo did not allow himself that sweet, sweet pleasure until Eleanor was writhing beneath him again and again. She appeared like a goddess with her peach colored hair fanning out over his pillow, cheeks flushed, lids hooded with passion.

For each time that she gave him pleasure, Viggo wanted to give her thrice as much.

Chapter 9

Viggo

"There is something I should have told you before tonight," Viggo murmured as they lay tangled in bed hours later. He couldn't understand why he was nervous to explain the bond. Perhaps because by omitting it, he felt as if he lied. When he told her there was no going back, she couldn't have known how serious that was.

She continued drawing circles on his skin with her fingertips, that sated smile still on her face. "Tell me."

"My kind doesn't marry."

Eleanor withdrew her hand. The hurt and surprise came instantly, and he regretted his choice of words. "You won't marry me? After—" That quickly her eyes were shimmering with tears. "I am a wretched fool, aren't I?" She threw the furs from her body and tried to climb over him and out of bed.

Viggo locked his arms around her waist and held her on top of him. "Wait, El."

"Let me go!" she demanded, squirming and making him all too aware of how easily he could be inside her again.

"You've misunderstood." He rolled, dropping her back down beside him and catching her with his legs.

"Why are you so strong?" She bucked her hips, doing nothing but enticing him even more.

"Eleanor." He meant for his tone to be chastising. Instead, he was purring, his tongue wetting his lips as he watched her thrumming pulse. "I'm going to marry you."

She stilled. "But you said—"

"I'm very lacking in my ability to communicate, as we've both learned. Give me a moment and I will explain." Viggo inhaled deeply, shuddering at how delicious she smelled. He shifted closer, drawing a line down the column of her throat with his nose. "My kind *do* get married, but only to keep up appearances. We do not find marriage to be a necessity because we have something much stronger between us and the women we love.

"*Drakonmein* will love once and only once. We have little choice over the woman we take as a mate. It is Lady Fate who decides for us, pairing us with a single woman from the moment we bond with her to the moment we both die."

"Doesn't Lady Fate decide for everyone?"

"It's different for me. I cannot be with another, even if I never found you or you rejected me and left me to live out my days alone. You are and always will be the only woman for me, Eleanor," he whispered along the shell of her ear. "Now that we have become one in flesh, I am bound to you."

She pushed his face away. "What does that mean?"

"Close your eyes." She did as he instructed. "Do you feel different?" He placed his hand over her heart, focusing on sending her as much love as he could through their bond. "Do you feel different here?"

Eleanor gasped. "What is that?"

"That is the bond between us. We are bound. You to me and me to you. My magic has tied us together eternally." Viggo held his breath, bracing for her reaction. Her face went blank, her emotions churning.

Then it was there. Elation.

"Magic? There is magic between us?" She grinned. "How does it work?"

He explained as best he could, not really sure how to answer the question because he didn't know how it worked. It was magic. There was often no logical explanation for it.

"Does this bond not please you?" She took his hand, eyes searching his face.

"I am so very pleased."

"Then why are you..." She closed her eyes, placing her other hand over her heart. "Whatever you are."

"There is more I haven't told you."

She shuttered herself a little, her shoulders hunched as she said, "Go on then."

"I knew what you were to me the moment you crested that hill."

"What I was to you?" Her nose demonstrated her confusion by wrinkling.

"My mate. I caught your scent on the wind years ago and I've been looking for you ever since. Imagine my surprise when you walked right up to my home."

This time her response was not as excited. "*Years* ago? How? Where were you looking for me?"

"You must have been in the Winter Wilds. I was flying over a stand of spruce and caught your scent. I followed it to Brula but never pinpointed where you were," he explained.

Eleanor's eyes widened. "When I was picking spruce tips. But how could you not find me? If you knew my scent, couldn't you track me through the streets of Brula?"

"I—" Well, yes, he could have, couldn't he? His own vehement denial of association with his family had kept him from her. "I couldn't."

"Why not?" Was that a touch of anger in her tone? "If I was made for you by Lady Fate and you made for me, why couldn't you search for me? Are you exiled from Brula? Is that why you won't go?"

"I'm not exiled, but I have my reasons for staying away." Reasons that were beginning to feel meager under her scrutiny. "I called for you. For weeks I called for you. You could have come to the Winter Wilds sooner." Though it was inherently dangerous, and she may not have made it to him unscathed.

"You called for me?" Eleanor sat up, a scowl crossing her face. "Is that what all that bellowing was? How was I to know what it meant? I don't speak dragon."

"You should have felt the pull. A mate is supposed to know a dragon's call."

"Well perhaps you have misidentified me because I didn't understand."

Viggo felt slapped. "You felt nothing when you heard me fill the night air with my song?"

"Not nothing." She averted her gaze. "It filled me with melancholy. I was never lonelier than the nights I could hear you. You always made me wish I could freely walk the Winter Wilds and seek some kind of peace that I couldn't name. But I knew better than to leave the city. You could have eaten me!"

"Sweet El." He caught her chin, lifting it so he could meet her velvety eyes. "I'm sorry I didn't come for you. That my search didn't take me through every inch of the capital streets. You are truly a treasure. The most beautiful gem I shall ever behold."

"Are you sure? That's not what you said when I asked to be your bride. There was something about proving myself and making me clean the filthy hole you live in." She rolled her eyes heavenward.

He latched his teeth onto the side of her neck and sucked until the skin was purple. "Jealousy makes me a petty man."

"Even then you were jealous? Of what?" She swatted playfully at him, giggling when his teeth moved lower, and his hands played notes on her ribs.

"That you gave yourself to another."

"I wouldn't have—"

He kissed the denial from her lips. "There's no use arguing the past. Now you're mine and you'll give yourself to no one else."

Eleanor smiled sweetly and twisted the ring on her left hand. "No one else."

Viggo kissed her again, opening her thighs and melding their bodies together once more.

"No one else," he repeated the promise to her. There would never be another for him.

CHAPTER 10

ELEANOR

H APPINESS WAS A FOREIGN and fleeting creature in Eleanor's life before Viggo. It wasn't that she was miserable through her every day, only that she was trudging. Each morning, she woke to hours of work, ready to do what it took to make sure she and her grandmama could continue living in Brula. Tiny moments of joy were all that she found to warm her heart through the winter.

One reckless jaunt through the Winter Wilds and all of that changed.

Mornings started not with chopping wood before the sun rose, but with a dip in the hot spring that bubbled below the cave Viggo called home. Eleanor would cook a hearty breakfast afterwards—assuming they didn't distract each other. Viggo offered her luxuries like she'd never seen before, but it was not spices from across the world or silken fabrics that wooed her. It was him.

She'd been with him no more than two months and already, she was hopelessly, wildly in love with him. The way he spoke in that seductive, purring tone gave her goosebump. His stories of travel and adventure left her sleepless as she pondered at the beauty of the world beyond Brula. And when they made love—which was often—she felt whole in a way she couldn't put words to. Eleanor felt as if she'd spent her life with a hole in her chest and hadn't realized until Viggo filled it.

The perfection of their days together distracted her for a time, but eventually the guilt began to gnaw at Eleanor. How long would three gold coins last her grandmama? They should have gotten her through the winter, at least. That was *years'* worth of salary that she'd pinched and hidden. Every solstice bonus tucked away for the future. But Grandmama was terrible with money and her vices would be the end of her.

Eleanor had everything Grandmama wanted for her—a husband to take care of her, a home to shelter her. Shouldn't she let the old woman know? Grandmama wasn't the kindest caretaker, but she kept Eleanor fed and housed as a child. She was owed an explanation, at least.

Viggo didn't seem to agree. "Your Grandmother's parting words were poison. Why should you go home to more venom?"

"She is the only family I have," Eleanor argued. "I'm responsible for making sure she is cared for."

"I am your family now." He encircled her waist with his arms, kissing her neck. "And you do not owe that woman anything. You never asked her to take you into her home."

That was where they differed. He spoke little of them, but Eleanor understood Viggo had dark feelings toward his family. It wasn't the same to him. They'd lived such very different lives—him raised in luxury, her raised on breadcrumbs and pinched coppers—and he couldn't grasp the sacrifices Grandmama made to keep her.

Eleanor left the conversation alone for a few days, pondering ways to get him to capitulate. She understood his reluctance to return to Brula, but at some point, he would have to face it. Especially if they were to marry. Wouldn't he want his family to know? They would have to find a high father and as far as she knew, there weren't many outside of the capital. Village dwellers from all over the country made early spring pilgrimages to be married in the temple in the center of the Brulian capital.

Winter was on the verge of retreat when the opportunity to go back to her old home came about.

"Tell me." Viggo teased, tickling her as she tried to fold the washing.

"I can't."

"Tell me who my enemy is so I can kill him."

Eleanor giggled. "Dragon or not, I'm fairly certain they will hunt you down if you kill the future king."

He became so still that it worried her. Even his breath seemed to cease, his heart quiet in his chest. "Jerome? It was Prince Jerome?"

Familiar shame burned her face. She stared intently at her hands. "Yes."

Viggo paced away, bracing his hand on the wall and leaning forward. He was quiet for a very long time, so long she felt as though he was punishing her with his silence. "Why? Why him?"

"He made me feel pretty when I was filthy. I thought that he liked the woman I am."

"Do you know—" He growled, slamming his palm into the stone. His voice was deep and angry when he continued. "Do you know what kind of man he is?"

"I do now." Eleanor turned to sit on a stone by the fire. Inside her the emotions were churning so fast she felt seasick. Viggo was furious and...was that disgust? Of course, it was. She'd given her virtue to a petulant prince in a cleaning closet. And now she was soiled. Eleanor should have known this was too good to be true. "I'm sorry."

"I think you should visit your Grandmama after all."

"You're...you're sending me away?"

"I'm giving you what you asked for," he answered flatly. "Tell me when you're ready."

Eleanor tried not to shed any tears as she took her folded dresses and stuffed them into Viggo's flying satchel, but there was no use holding it in. At least she didn't have an audience. Viggo left soon after asking her to pack, flying into the sky and making her wonder if he truly was taking her to Brula.

This seemed like a parting, and she didn't know how to process it. How could such happiness sour so quickly? How could what he claimed was burning, enduring, infinite love be snuffed out by something so insignificant? Men were rarely pure of flesh when *they* made a marriage match. Why was it so different for women?

Eleanor tucked her trunk of spices into the bag and a hunk of dry cheese, too. Grandmama would be thrilled by both. Perhaps it would quell some of her anger when she discovered Eleanor wasn't kidnapped or eaten by a dragon.

Too fast, her few belongings were packed and ready for a night—or many nights—in Brula. She stood at the mouth of the cave and called out, "I'm ready, Viggo."

The dragon appeared like corporeal mist coming down from the clouds. His clawed hands dipped into the cave, snatching Eleanor up so fast her head whipped back. With a startled scream she gripped at his scaly arms, terrified he would drop her in his anger. Surely, he didn't hate her enough to kill her?

Gods, even thinking that he hated her made Eleanor break down into tears all over again. Somehow the bond had gone quiet, as if Viggo was holding himself back from her.

The flight to the edge of the wilds was cold and swift. Viggo circled the trees, searching for a clearing big enough for his landing. He set Eleanor gently in the snow, shifting and turning to her without meeting her eyes. "My clothes."

She had packed a set for him because she'd hoped she was wrong about his feelings, but she hadn't really expected he would want them. "You're coming with me?"

"Did you think I would let my mate walk the Winter Wilds and enter the city alone?" He snapped.

"I—I suppose not."

That was the last they spoke as they quietly journeyed from the forest and onto the main road. During the day the gates to the city were open for the travelers and traders that came from villages and cities further north. Viggo and Eleanor walked through them easily enough, though the guards did a double take when they spotted Viggo. Tall and imposing as he was, just about every person they passed gave him a second look.

Eleanor bristled when the first woman carrying a basket of bread offered Viggo a coquettish smile. By the fourth time, she was stomping to her grandmama's home.

Today was probably the worst day of her life. Women in pretty dresses were fawning over Viggo and he did nothing to discourage it. Now she was about to show him the filthy hovel where she grew up and it would probably be the place they parted ways.

I will not cry again, she told herself.

"Grandmama?" Eleanor knocked as she opened the door to their tiny home. "Are you home?"

The air was no warmer inside than it was out. No embers sparkled in the hearth and there wasn't the faintest scent of food. Fearing the worst, Eleanor rushed inside and flung open the door to Grandmama's bedroom. The bed was unmade and things from her chest were scattered about—as they often were—but the old woman was not lying dead on her sheets.

Viggo hurried after her, filling the doorway and gruffly asking, "What's the matter?"

"I—Gods—I worried my Grandmama was dead. She's clearly not been here for a while."

"No one has been here for many days."

"How can you tell?" Eleanor skirted around him and studied the kitchen. There was not a scrap of food to be found.

"The scents are very stale."

"Maybe she found someone to take her in. The temple sometimes feeds the elderly and the poor." Grandmama was always too proud for that. Perhaps her pride withered with Eleanor gone. "You don't have to stay. I'll wait for her here and if she doesn't arrive home by this evening, I'll go speak to the neighbors."

Viggo cracked both knuckles and sank into one of the too small chairs around the table. "I won't leave you alone in this foul and degenerate city."

She studied him, shocked not only by the venomous way he spoke but what he said. "You aren't leaving me?"

His scowl was dark, the darkest expression she'd ever seen color his handsome face. "We are bound." That wasn't particularly reassuring.

"Then what are we doing here?"

Viggo rubbed his face and groaned. "It was the alternative."

"To what?"

"Taking to the skies and flying until my anger dissipated. Taking to the skies and burning the whole capital to the ground."

Eyes downcast, she murmured, "If I had known you were out there waiting for me, I never would have…"

"Come here, El." Eleanor took the chair across from him. "Closer." She scooted her chair around the table. "Closer." A squeak left her when she was yanked from her chair and into his lap. "That's better."

She closed her eyes, leaning her face against his jaw. "I thought you were leaving me here."

"I am angry, Eleanor, but not with you. I'm angry that disgusting rat dared put his hands on my mate." There was that venom again. Why was Viggo filled with such hate?

"You know him."

His sigh was heavy with regret. "We were thick as thieves once. My brother too."

A face suddenly popped into her head. The eyes were a darker blue, the hair a darker shade of blonde, but the angular, cat-like features and broad shoulders were the same. It was not often that Jerome was seen without Mikael Nordin at his side. *That* was where Eleanor had seen the crest. Mikael was aloof at best, snobbish and rude at his worst. She avoided even looking at him if she could, not daring to provoke some cruel remark from him.

"Mikael Nordin?"

"So, you've had the pleasure of meeting my dear baby brother."

"I wouldn't call it a pleasure."

"He has become an insufferable brat over the years. Jerome as well. I'm ashamed to admit that I was not so different from them once." Viggo traced a deep groove in the imperfect wood of the tabletop. "We wasted many summers together, drinking and sailing and...indulging in other ways."

She recalled the woman on the boat and his vague mention of indulgences. "Indulging?"

"There are many things a *Drakonmein* can do with a woman that will not bind them. My brother discovered this during our first drunken summer on Jerome's houseboat. Prince Jerome has varying taste in women and enjoys the company of many."

Perhaps she didn't have the right to be jealous, but it still burned her throat when she asked, "Did you...discover these things too?"

"I drank myself into a stupor every night for weeks. That is all. I will admit, I watched. Jerome likes to have an audience and to cause humiliation in those he views as lesser than him. I became numb to his depravity." He shifted uncomfortably beneath her. "But I wanted a mate. I planned to wait an eternity for her if I had to. Eventually, I came to see the life we were leading for what it was. No woman would want a drunk lord's son. No mate would want a man who sat by and watched as women were used and discarded, children created and disowned."

"Children?"

"I know for certain that Jerome has left at least one bastard without a father. He is not the only man in court who has. Their dalliances are well known, as are the children born of their indiscretions. It is not even the worst of their sins. *That* is why I do not come to Brula. That is why I cannot be here, Eleanor."

She chewed her bottom lip. "You don't have to stay. But I can't leave without knowing what happened to my Grandmama."

Viggo set her back in her chair and fixed his gaze on the narrow window in the kitchen. The sky was pale and cold. She knew how he longed for it. The hunch in his shoulders told of his distaste for this place. Eleanor could understand the oppressiveness. She'd lived with it all her life, lived as one of those Jerome and his courtiers considered lesser.

"I will be all right. You can return for me at dusk."

"I can't leave you here. This city is built on malicious intentions."

Eleanor wrapped her arms around his neck. "You're being a bit dramatic. I've lived here all my life and nothing terrible has ever happened to me."

He glowered his disagreement. "Do you plan to go looking for your Grandmama in some secret gambling ring? And what about the prince?"

"I will speak to the neighbors and search the temple. The prince will hardly be wandering around with beggars." She was quickly winning, she could tell. He was practically scratching his skin off. Viggo really, truly hated Brula. Eleanor hadn't realized it would torment him so or else she might not have asked him to come here.

"You will be right here when I return at dusk?"

"In this very chair, if it pleases you."

"Believe me, El, when I promise that this city will burn if I come to find you are not here *and* unharmed."

She kissed him once, twice, then a third time because she couldn't help herself. "I believe you. Now stop worrying and set yourself free."

Viggo added a fourth to their kiss before vanishing. The back door was still open as he raced to the wall. Eleanor wasn't sure if he waited until he was out of the city before shifting forms. She was too distracted by the sudden banging of the front door against the wall to care.

"Eleanor! Thank the Gods! You really are here!" Kara Lockler, the wife of a neighboring farmer, crossed the short distance to the kitchen and took her hands. "We thought perhaps you'd been taken too."

"Taken? Why would I be taken? Who would take me?"

"Where have you been? You haven't heard?"

"I've been—" There really was no explaining where she'd been without sounding mad. "I'm getting married. I've been making arrangements."

"Married?" Kara noticed the ring on Eleanor's finger for the first time. "To who? Gods, look at that sparkle!" She lifted Eleanor's hand to examine the jewelry.

Eleanor dropped Kara's hands and stood. "What's going on? Where is my Grandmama?"

Kara's complexion lightened, and she swallowed audibly. "Right. I've forgotten myself. Your Grandmama is in the dungeons."

"*What*? Why would she be there? She's a frail old woman!"

"When you left we all thought you'd been stolen. Even this far north there are slavers, y'know. They smuggle women out through the port." Kara took Viggo's empty seat at the table. "Your Grandmama searched half the city for you. When no one had word of you, she went to the king for aid. I don't know what she thought they were going to do for her. She must've offended them terribly. That Mary said she saw your Grandmama being dragged through the castle, yelling something about her reward."

"That's not right." Eleanor stomped her foot. "What kind of self-important king imprisons an old woman over a simple offense? Oaf! That whole family is full of selfish buffoons."

"Watch your tongue, Eleanor!" Kara warned. "You mustn't let people hear you talk like that, or you'll be joining your Grandmama."

"Good. I'll be doing that right now." Eleanor was well and done with the royal family of Brula.

"You only just got here. Where is your groom?"

"I'm going to see about getting my Grandmama out. As for my groom, I don't know where he is. The man can be very mercurial." Eleanor took Kara's hand and led her to the door.

"But—" Kara hesitated as Eleanor guided her out, clearly more interested in resolving her curiosity than being helpful.

"I'll return home soon enough and tell you all about my future husband," she promised as she nearly slammed the door in Kara's face.

Grandmama was in the dungeon. *The dungeon!* What kind of king threw an old woman in the dungeon? She intended to find out.

The problem, she realized, was that Viggo wanted nothing to do with the court or the royal family. He would be furious if he knew what she was planning. But Grandmama was her only family. Eleanor had come to ensure she was faring well on her own. Clearly, she wasn't.

It would only be for a moment. Just long enough to convince the king or whoever would speak to her to let Grandmama go.

Yes. Only a moment. It would be that simple.

CHAPTER 11

ELEANOR

THE WALK TO THE castle was a familiar one, the cobblestone road a quiet companion beneath her feet. Though Eleanor marched to and from the castle each day for years, the journey was different somehow. Perhaps because *she* was different. Her time in the Winter Wilds made her bolder. Surer of herself. Certain of what she wanted and what she was willing to give to attain it.

That was why she felt confident marching through the front gates and skipping the servant's entrance to come into the main hall. Two guards gave her suspicious looks, but they recognized her and didn't stop her from entering. They were, however, clearly confused by her attire. She was wearing something closer to a rag than a dress the last she was seen here. Her attire now was much finer, though still a bit dirty from flying.

Yes, life had certainly changed for Eleanor since the beginning of winter.

Viggo would be displeased when he learned of where she was and what she was doing. Eleanor had no choice. Grandmama might be a bitter woman with a gambling habit and a permanent scowl, but she didn't deserve to fester and freeze in a dungeon.

The throne room was empty this time of day, the king busy meeting with his advisors while the queen was likely tittering away with some courtier wives as they planned the next royal event. Her target was a creature of habit as much as his parents and Eleanor suspected she would find him exactly where she always did when he was finished breaking his fast.

Stone walls echoed the click of her boot heels. Torches and candles whipped about as fire dodged the wind kicked up by her determined pace. Eleanor was turning the corner to the library so swiftly that she nearly collided with Mary. Her friend was tousled, braid frizzy and coming undone, her skirts out of place. Mary hurriedly smoothed the garment down and wiped the back of her hand across her mouth, looking guilty.

"Ellie! Gods! What are you doing here? We've all been so worried about you!" Eleanor dodged Mary, not wanting to be touched by hands that had obviously been in places she would rather forget.

Prince Jerome was a length away, readjusting his pants as casually as if he was in his private chamber. Smug satisfaction was perched unbecomingly on his face. Wooing lowly maids was some kind of game to him, it would seem. Eleanor wanted to slap the gratification from his face. How had she ever found that lecher of a man charming or handsome?

"Don't be angry with me, Eleanor," Mary whispered apologetically. "I only wanted to know if royal cock was better."

"And?" Eleanor arched an incredulous brow.

"He was rough," her friend admitted. "And quick."

"He's a pig, Mary, and he will take advantage of you."

"Shhh, Eleanor! You mustn't speak like that."

Eleanor ignored her, pushing forward to grab the prince's attention. "Prince Jerome! Why is my Grandmama in your dungeon?"

As she walked to the castle, Eleanor had decided she wouldn't be following customs and groveling to get information from Jerome or his father. Let them lock her away in the dungeon with her grandmama. Viggo would come for her if they did, and probably toast them all before setting her free. It was apparent from their parting conversation that Viggo would enjoy it.

Jerome glanced up, a scowl forming on his face for only a heartbeat until he realized who it was that spoke. His eyes widened, and he quickly finished readjusting his outfit before offering a welcoming hand. "Thank the Gods. We've been searching everywhere for you!"

She halted in her angry march, taken aback by his demeanor. "For me? Why? What have you done to my Grandmama?"

"Your Grandmother? That woman who stole you away? Have no fear, we have her in custody."

"I know. That's why I'm here. What do you mean stole me away?"

Jerome reached for her hand, but she jerked back. He shot a wrathful look over Eleanor's shoulder. The sound of Mary's quick retreat followed.

Pig.

"You truly don't know? Of course, you don't. How could you with that woman lying to you all your life? Please, come with me. There's so much to tell you." Again, he tried for her hand and again she avoided his touch.

"Is this some kind of trick?"

"No trick. You are a very special guest in this castle. My father would like to meet with you, my lady."

Eleanor's curiosity won out over her caution. With a bemused face, she nodded her chin. "I should like an audience with the king."

Jerome was in quite the hurry as he guided Eleanor through the long hallway past the library and to the king's private study. Her courage waned a little more with each step and her palms began to sweat. Why would the King of Brula want an audience with her? How did he even know who she was? She'd seen him only a handful of times during her employment in the castle and he had never acknowledged her existence.

"What's this about?" Eleanor questioned just before Jerome lifted a hand to knock.

"You'll understand soon."

"Are you going to throw me in your dungeon too? Has my Grandmama committed such a heinous crime?"

"Gods, no, my lady! Your Grandmama has committed a treasonous crime. But you? You are the innocent in all of this." Jerome patted her shoulder in an attempt at reassurance. Her stomach roiled at the contact. "Don't fret, sweet lady."

"I'm not a lady," she mumbled, steeling herself when the king beckoned for them to enter.

"Father?" The prince's countenance shifted even more, his face becoming stern and his voice just a touch uncertain. Eleanor rather liked the thought of Jerome feeling timid.

"Jerome? What is it now? I'm in the middle of reviewing this—"

"I've brought company, your highness." Jerome bugged his eyes out and made a face. "I've located the princess."

King Brennard abruptly lifted his face from the parchment before him, the movement making the candelabra on his desk rattle. The surprised expression smoothed some of the stress that usually lined his eyes, straightening his chronically displeased moue into a set of lips that matched his son's. Father and son shared many of the same characteristics, right down to their inability to select one woman and stick with her, if rumors were to be believed.

"The princess?" He eyed her with a look bordering on disgust. "Are you certain this is her?"

"Very." Jerome's nod was exaggerated.

"Of course! The princess! Do come in, dear."

At the last minute Eleanor remembered to curtsy, stumbling awkwardly back onto her feet as she glanced between the prince and the king. "Your highness, thank you for granting me an audience, but I'm terribly confused. I haven't come about a princess. I'm here for my Grandmama. Why is she in your dungeon?"

King Brennard scowled as if he meant to chastise her, discouraging himself at the last minute and calmly saying, "That woman is a criminal. That's why she is in the dungeon. Please, have a seat." He pointed to a plush chair near the hearth.

A king did not offer a seat to one of his maids. This wasn't right. "What's going on?" She asked, ignoring the request to sit.

"Elisa—"

"My name is Eleanor."

"Er, not exactly. You see, you have a family that is very eager for your return. Are you familiar with Yore?"

She conjured an image of the map hanging in the library. Once or twice, she had glanced at it, but with no ability to read, the countries and kingdoms meant little to her.

"I have heard the name."

The king canted his head to the side, smiling in a manner that was at once sly and feigned amiability. "Would it surprise you to know that you were born there?"

"Not really. I haven't the slightest idea where I was born or where my mother was from. She could be Gazari for all I know."

"She is certainly not Gazari."

Jerome came up behind her, placing his hands on her shoulders. "She is a queen. And you are a princess."

Chapter 12

Eleanor

ELEANOR WAS SEATED IN the plushest chair she'd ever used. It was so comfortable, in fact, that she felt like squirming. The luxury seemed wrong and out of place contrasting with the shock that was still moving through her in tiny tremors.

She wanted to believe it was a dream or perhaps a cruel joke. But why would the king of Brula do such a petty thing? And to a commoner of no consequence?

Long ago, when she was barely older than seven, she remembered hearing the story of the missing princess of Yore. She was the only daughter born to the king and queen, precious for that alone. The royal family of Yore was discussing a betrothal with a neighboring kingdom when a trusted servant snatched her away. As far as anyone knew, there was never a request for a ransom. The family received no threats. Princess Elisa was simply gone without a trace.

When Eleanor mentioned the story to her grandmama, asking if anyone ever found the poor princess, she was given a beating with a rolling pin. Grandmama was insistent that she never, *never* bring the story up again. Eleanor had always assumed it was because the tale made her grandmama sad.

Such a naive girl. Always so gullible.

The truth, it turned out, was because the story made her grandmama bitter. Her grandmama who wasn't her grandmama at all, but the mother of the man who kidnapped the princess of Yore. When he didn't get the ransom he was hoping for, he brought the infant to his mother and demanded she care for the girl.

Eleanor supposed she was lucky that Grandmama wasn't the kind of woman to dump an unwanted child in the Winter Wilds, else she wouldn't be here to feel the anger and sorrow and confusion that were troubling her now.

"You mean to tell me that I have a family that wants me? Parents that would like to see me returned to them?"

"Yes," the king answered with a touch of exasperation. To be fair, Eleanor had asked the same question in so many words at least three times.

"More importantly," said Jerome, kneeling in front of her. "You're a princess."

"I don't really care about that." Eleanor shrunk back as he attempted to grasp her hands. She would be happy to never touch him again.

Perhaps once not so long ago the thought of being a princess would thrill her. But only because wealth and luxury seemed more desirable than useless toil. Now she had Viggo and the life they were building together was as luxurious as she needed.

"I still don't understand how you can know this for certain. If the princess was an infant when she went missing, no one would know what she looked like today."

"How old are you?" The king prompted.

"Twenty one."

"And when is your birthday?"

"The third day of spring."

That sly smile painted his face again. "Just like princess Elisa." He opened a drawer in his desk and tugged out a weathered, white baby blanket, turning it so a hand stitched rose with a sword dashing through it was visible. "Do you recognize this?"

Only because she had seen it on crates of goods when she was bartering with the sailors at the docks. "Not really."

"When you went missing, your Grandmama came to us with this blanket and the story we've just shared. She claimed you were the princess of Yore and that she needed help to search for you. Until her story is proven false, which I do not believe it will be, she will stay imprisoned for her role in your kidnapping."

"My kidnapping," Eleanor murmured, trying to wrap her head around it all.

"I have already written to the king and queen of Yore. They would be delighted to know that we have found you. Since my letter arrived, they have been preparing for your return, praying to the Gods for your safety." The king ran a hand over the blanket to straighten it. "I can arrange for your journey as soon as tomorrow afternoon."

"Tomorrow?" No, she couldn't just leave. What about Viggo? She needed to tell him what was happening. They would have to go together. Eleanor didn't want to visit Yore, wherever that was, without him. "But I can't just leave! And what about my—about the woman who raised me? I would like to speak to her."

"Nonsense. She's a liar and a criminal."

"She kept me alive! I can't let her rot in a dungeon. Not without hearing the truth from her lips."

It was surreal to argue with the King of Brula—*the King*—and not fear any repercussions. Eleanor fussed until he begrudgingly agreed to allow her to visit her grandmama—with the company of Jerome and two guards. She wasn't keen on the company of anyone, but it seemed she was all but a prisoner herself now that the prince had identified her. She wouldn't easily be allowed to leave.

One of the guards that clinked and thumped down the cold stone staircase to the lower portion of the castle was a familiar face. Hansen, Eleanor remembered, was shy, polite, and particularly fond of Mary. She cast a scathing glance at Jerome and his princely face, wondering if he cared at all that Hansen would never ask for Mary's hand in marriage if he knew that she'd been with the prince.

A sudden cold fear gripped her insides. Was Viggo rethinking his proposal now that he knew of Eleanor's brief affair with Prince Jerome? He'd been distant ever since he learned the truth, even his emotions felt muted in the bond between them.

Metal groaned as one of the guards opened a steel gate and led the way down a long, torch-lit hall. It was dim and damp, very poor accommodations for an old woman. Her concern for her grandmama, despite what the king claimed, had her momentarily forgetting her fears about Viggo.

"How long has she been down here?" Eleanor demanded, pointing an accusing finger at Jerome.

His eyes narrowed a fraction. "Three weeks."

"Three weeks? The air down here is frigid! She could freeze to death. Who is caring for her?"

"The guards care for all the prisoners." Jerome sounded as if he was trying to keep the boredom from his tone. Deflowering maids in cleaning closets was more entertaining than actual royal duties, it seemed. "She is alive," he added as an afterthought.

"Despicable," Eleanor muttered, hurrying past the lead guard and asking, "Where is she?"

But she didn't need his response because in answer to her echoing words, a throaty voice croaked, "Eleanor? Is that you, girl?"

A wizened hand reached through the bars in a cell near the end of the hall. Eleanor rushed to grasp it, passing the murmurs and snores of other prisoners. Grandmama's hands were icy and rough, her skin nearly translucent.

"Grandmama! It's me. Are you all right?"

"Do I look all right, you twit? They've imprisoned me for trying to find you! I'm starving and my bones have turned brittle from the cold." Gentle as always, her grandmama.

At her sharp tone, Eleanor pulled her hand away. Fixing her eyes on those dark, bitter irises she'd grown to know so well. "Is it true? What they say about me being the Princess of Yore?"

"I can't say if it's true or not. I don't know what they've told you." Grandmama crossed her arms stubbornly.

"Grandmama." Eleanor wanted to snarl. "For once in your life be honest with me. Am I your granddaughter? Or am I a daughter of Yore?"

"You're no blood of mine!" she spat. "Not with those lazy hands. Now get me out of here and prove a lifetime of kindness and generosity from me wasn't wasted!"

"All this time," Eleanor whispered. "All this time you knew I had family. I had a future. Why didn't you tell me? Why did you wait so long to come to the royal family with the truth?"

"The King of Yore refused to pay the ransom my son demanded! Why would the Brulian bastard be any different? If you thought you were mine, at least there was someone to look after me when I grew old. Or there should have been if you hadn't thrown away your virtue and dawdled in your search for a husband."

Humiliation bloomed on Eleanor's face, and she did her best to pretend the three men witnessing the exchange weren't there. "But why did you reveal the truth when I was gone?"

"You left me with scraps! How was I to care for myself on three gold coins? I needed the king to find you. I couldn't have you running off to leave me on my deathbed."

"You've already spent the coins?" She sputtered. "Three gold coins could get us through a year, Grandmama! And you aren't dying! You mean old hag! You will live to be one hundred years old out of spite." She swiped angrily beneath her eyes, refusing to shed a tear in front of the prince. "I can't believe you lied to me. You made me believe I was unwanted by my parents, orphaned, and with no one in the world but you."

"You think this prince doesn't want to use you as much as the rest of them? You were useless until now. Your father wouldn't even pay for your safe return. You are *unwanted*, girl, except for the husband you can now acquire, and the story of a missing princess found that will bring people bowing at your father's feet. Does it feel better to be a pawn in their game?" Grandmama pressed her wicked face up to the bars. "Well? Does it? You'll wear what they tell you and wed who they tell you and bear children when they tell you. You will be nothing but what they make of you."

"I will never be nothing," Eleanor hissed through her teeth. "And I will never be unwanted again." Deep in her chest she reached for that place where she felt the new and comforting bond with Viggo. Even if he was distant and quiet, his presence soothed her pain enough to smooth her expression as she turned to Jerome. "Release her, please. Bring my request to your father if you need. She is an old woman, and she will die down here. There is no use imprisoning her."

"Good girl," Grandmama crooned. "I knew you were my good girl."

"Whether you die in here or out there, you will die alone, Grandmama. You have made sure of it."

Eleanor held her breath as she pivoted on her heel and marched back down the long, haunting halls of the dungeon. One or two prisoners called out to her, this time awake and aware enough to shout pleas or lewd comments. She ignored them. There was no more room inside of her for any distaste, grief, or uncertainty. Like an overfilled wine cup, she was brimming with emotion, and it threatened to slosh over in a spray of tears with every step.

Leave the castle and get home. Find Viggo and get home. That was Eleanor's mission, and she was determined.

That mission only got her to the top of the ridiculously long flight of stairs before Jerome waylaid her. "Princess! Wait! Where are you going?"

"Home."

"Yes, tomorrow, but for now my father has offered you generous accommodations. I can have one of my mother's servants show you there now."

"No, thank you, your highness, I'm going to my home."

He frowned. "Don't you live in a hovel?"

Eleanor frowned back, realizing she had inadvertently followed him deeper into the castle. "A cave, actually."

"You there!" Jerome boomed to a woman down the hall. "Come show the princess to a guest room."

"I can't stay here. The man I am engaged to is waiting for me."

The woman scurried toward them, shoulders at her ears and eyes wide when she recognized Eleanor. Her name escaped Eleanor, but her mousy face and timid posture were familiar. "Of course, your highness. This way, my lady."

"And have someone draw her a bath. She'll need fresh clothing and food as well. Do everything you must to make her comfortable."

"Wait, but I'm supposed to go—"

"Don't fret, my lady, we will see to all your needs."

Eleanor trotted helplessly within the pack of servants that somehow appeared around her. It was as if they melted through the walls the way a ghost would, surrounding her in some strange babbling cage. They tittered and fussed over her hair and her dress before she'd even made it anywhere private.

And once they were behind closed doors? Eleanor was stripped of her garments before she could protest. One girl tried to remove the ring that Viggo gave her, but Eleanor quickly snatched her hand away.

"It will be ruined in the bath, my lady."

"It will be fine. I don't need a bath." She tried to cover herself. Was this what courtiers went through every day? It was humiliating.

"Nonsense, my lady. The water is already warm."

"No!" Eleanor snatched her dress back from one of the ladies and tugged it over her head. The ties on the side were lose, and she was without any undergarments. She didn't care. "I haven't asked for any of this. Please leave me."

Reluctantly, the clucking flock of ladies vacated the room. Eleanor huffed out a breath and looked around her. Fire sparkled in a massive hearth. A deep tub steamed in the corner nearest the fireplace. From there to the bed was double the length of her entire home. It was more than ostentatious.

Fluffy pink pillows littered every surface and silky fabrics hung all over. Why was the fabric hanging around the bed? To give a woman privacy from her brazen servants? Perhaps. Otherwise, they might braid her hair while she was sleeping or do something equally violating and strange.

For much of her life Eleanor dreamed of such luxury, if only to escape the hard, bitter work she had to do to survive. Now it felt wrong, suffocating in comparison to the eclectic space Viggo shared with her.

Viggo. Gods, he had to be worried. Through the window Eleanor could see the sun sinking below the walls of the city, the last tendrils of golden light already retiring until late the next morning.

Was he worried? Searching the bond between them, she felt little. Was she too overwhelmed to discern his emotions from hers?

Apparently, yes, she was missing the anxious anger floating from him to her, because not a moment later she heard the familiar trumpet of a dragon. Only this time, he wasn't miles away flying over the Winter Wilds. He was right above the castle.

Somewhere outside her door a woman screamed. Men shouted and footsteps echoed down the hall. She'd been right to think Viggo would come for her. He had.

Now she needed to reach him before he followed her lead and did something truly reckless.

There was a guard stationed outside her door. Whether it was to keep her in, keep others out, or protect her from the roving dragon, Eleanor couldn't say.

Well, only one way to find out.

Once her clothes were righted and her boots tied, Eleanor flung the chamber door open and stomped into the hall. If she was supposed to be a princess, she would act like one. Or try to, anyway.

"My lady, where are you going?" The guard's footsteps echoed hers.

"Er, out."

"There's a dragon about!" Over her shoulder she glanced at him. He couldn't be older than nineteen, face pale and youthful. Perhaps that would play to her advantage.

"Yes, I know. How terrible." They stared at each other for a long moment. "That's why I'm going out." She hesitated, not wanting to get the young man in trouble. "I have to speak with the king. I was meant to be safe here and now there's a dragon? Unacceptable."

"My lady, you are safe here. I promise you. The prince has instructed me to lay down my life to protect you."

"Well, please don't do that. I'm overriding his command." Could she do that?

"My lady—" He faltered, clearly torn between following her as she took backward steps and obeying her order. Poor boy.

"Stay here. I'm all right. I just need to see the king."

"But—" Eleanor whirled as fast as her dress allowed, running down the hall and aiming for a narrow staircase she knew would bring her to the kitchen. "My lady, please wait!"

She ignored the many pleas from the young guard, hoping it would not cost him too dearly if the prince came looking for her and she was gone. The stairs were treacherous at this speed, and she nearly slipped and cracked her skull twice. At the bottom she collided with a maid carrying a tray of tea. Porcelain shattered and skittered along the floor.

"Look what you've done! Watch where you're—Eleanor?"

Eleanor didn't stop to see who it was that recognized her. The dragon bellowed again, and she picked up her pace, dodging cooks and stumbling over a bag of potatoes as she headed for the kitchen door. The cold air bit at her sweat drenched skin when she burst into the night.

"I'm here!" Eleanor shouted as loudly as she dared, racing across the castle grounds and toward the bridge that connected with the main road.

She skidded to a stop when she saw the main gates were closed. Of course, they were. The gates were always closed after nightfall. Thinking on her feet, she changed her trajectory to the port door where servants came and went. There would be a guard stationed there, perhaps two, but it should be easy enough to pass them. They would recognize her.

The sole guard at the servant's entrance was surprised by her appearance—she did look much different now that she wasn't filthy—but he didn't make much effort to stop her.

"The dragon has left the Wilds! He's somewhere overhead!" As he said it, he ducked into the doorway, flattening himself against the wall as best he could.

"I'm sure he's harmless!" Eleanor shouted over her shoulder as she ran through the doorway.

The narrow path along the castle walls that led to the road was hard to navigate in the dark. She took it as fast as she dared, occasionally glancing up to see if there was any sign of Viggo. He'd gone quiet, and it was impossible to spot him in the gloaming.

"I'm going home!" She shouted when she made it to the road, hoping he would hear her.

Stars glittered overhead by the time the first row of buildings were in sight. A bakery glowed warm to her right and a seamstress shop was rising to her left. The sudden absence of those twinkling lights was the only warning Eleanor received before a great shadow dropped down over her. Claws encircled her body and with a painful jolt she was rocketed into the air.

Viggo's scales were so warm they might have been unbearable if she wasn't frozen down to the bone. She pressed one cheek against him where he held her and curled in on herself as much as she could.

No amount of dragon warmth could keep the dagger sharp winter winds at bay. By the time they passed over the city and drew near the cave entrance, Eleanor had gone numb. Her teeth even ceased chattering, the muscles in her jaw too cold to tremble. Viggo dumped her on her feet in the dark cave. Her knees buckled, and she cried out when the stone slammed into her joints.

"Eleanor!" Viggo was there, lifting her into his arms. She embraced him, trying to drink in the scalding heat of him.

As quickly as it began, the embrace ended. Eleanor was once again dropped from his hold—this time onto the bed—and he vanished. The cave was far too dark for her to see where he was or what he was doing.

An explosive burst of flame cleared up any confusion as the fire came to life, blessed heat dancing toward her. She slipped from the bed, taking one of the furs with her, and huddling before the fire.

"Thank you."

Viggo didn't answer. He shoved his legs into a pair of trousers then stood across the fire from her, his face inscrutable. There was a spark in his eyes she didn't recognize, some emotion that seemed too bitter to match his playful demeanor. Searching the bond, she finally found all the feelings that hadn't been clear to her—rage, fear, and...jealousy?

"You went to the castle."

As she had promised she wouldn't. Eleanor conveniently forgot that promise when she realized her grandmama—that woman—was in peril. "I'm sorry. I shouldn't have, but my Grandmama needed my help. Or I thought she did."

"Your Grandmama?" He scoffed. "You can do better than that."

She gaped. "Are you accusing me of something?"

"Did you see him?"

Guilt unfurled in her middle. "Not on purpose."

"Did he touch you?" His pupils became slits, his voice shifting until each word was a vicious shard of ice.

"No—I mean, he put his hand on my shoulder. Nothing happened with the prince, Viggo. Don't you trust me?"

His silence stretched for far too long. "Tell me why you were there."

"Only if you sit with me. I haven't done anything to betray your trust. I never would." She lifted one side of the fur and motioned for him to join her. "My love is yours alone." Eleanor wanted to be offended that he could think so poorly of her, but she understood. Beneath his anger was a tight and uncomfortable pain. She imagined she would feel the same if she knew of a lover that came before her.

Viggo surrendered, dropping to the floor with a dramatic huff. She slipped her thighs over his, settling into his lap and resting her face on his chest. Instantly his arms were around her, holding her so tight she could scarcely breathe.

"I was so worried about you, El. You didn't come back."

"I'm sorry. I wasn't thinking clearly. So much has happened since this morning."

"Tell me."

She told him everything, starting from the moment she walked out of Grandmama's home and ending with her escape from the castle. With every sentence Viggo tensed beneath her, his muscles winding so tightly he felt the same as the surrounding stone.

"I have a family," she murmured, still reeling from the shock and wonder. "Do you think it's true? Have you ever heard of the Princess of Yore?"

"I remember her story. It was a tragedy." He shook his head. "That princess is likely dead."

"But *I* am her!"

"Because your lying, stealing Grandmother told you so?"

Eleanor scowled, scooting from his lap. "You don't believe me?"

"I don't believe them. There is no way to prove it."

"But the blanket—"

"Is only that." Viggo stood and aggressively dropped another log onto the fire. "Your Grandmother could have purchased it from a traveling merchant or stolen it. She could have made it herself to fool the royal family."

"And what if she didn't?" Eleanor wanted to do a bit of her own log throwing. The day was long, and she was tired down to her soul. "The King and Queen of Yore are expecting to meet me. King Brennard has arranged travel for me tomorrow."

"*What?* You're going to leave?"

"Not without you. I thought you could come with me. You are to be my husband. It would be right for you to meet my family."

"No."

"No?" Somehow the word didn't quite make sense. Surely, he wasn't denying her the chance to meet her parents—parents she believed never wanted her.

"I won't be trapped in the suffocating hell of royal affairs."

"But Viggo, they're my family!"

"I am supposed to be your family," he hissed.

"What is wrong with you?" Eleanor stood, throwing the fur from her shoulders and pointing angrily at him. "All of my life I was told that I am worthless. That I had a mother who wanted to leave me to the wolves and a father who left me on my Grandmama's table with barely a word. I believed that I was wanted by no one."

"But you know that is not true now, because I want you. You are mine."

"You say that as if it is all that should matter."

"It is."

"Viggo, my family matters to me."

He tossed his hands up. "Strangers! How can you say strangers matter to you?"

Suddenly there were tears welling in her eyes again. "How can you say they shouldn't?"

"I can't be a part of this ridiculous scheme. I promised myself that I would never return to that life."

"To what life? What are you saying?"

"You know where I come from."

"And I want to know where I come from. Don't you miss them? Your parents?"

"Those people are despicable, and I will not associate myself with them."

"But they're your family!"

"No, you are my family. I need only my mate." He stretched to pick a shirt from a pile of garments by the fire, tugging it over his head.

"You truly won't come with me?"

He looked up sharply, his eyes once again became those stormy dragon eyes. "You would still go? Without me?"

Her voice was small. "I have to know them. To see them."

"You would leave me?"

"I am not leaving you. I only wish to see their faces, to know the sound of my mother and father's voices."

Viggo stared at her for a very, very long time. In her chest she felt a strange tingling, then nothing. It was as if the bond was a door between them and he had just closed it in her face. "Very well. I shall return you to Brula tomorrow."

"Viggo..."

"Get some rest. You will need it for your journey. Yore is a day by boat, further on horseback."

"Viggo wait—" In one breath he shifted from man to dragon, stretching his great wings and leaping from the cave.

Eleanor added extra logs to the fire before curling beneath the furs. No amount of heat warmed her. She felt numb from the inside out. How could he be so callous? After listening to her whisper her secret dreams of finding her mother and meeting her father.

His dismissal hurt almost as much as his physical absence. She lay awake for most of the night, longing for him, cursing him, wishing she knew what to do with him.

Chapter 13

Eleanor

Viggo still had scales when Eleanor woke tired and stiff the next morning. He was curled at the entrance to the cave, watching her with those sharp dragon eyes. She murmured a good morning to him and wasn't surprised when he didn't respond. This was all too good to be true. Lady Fate had no love for Eleanor and decided long ago that she could only be allowed so much happiness before it soured.

It wasn't her plan to choose between Viggo and her newly discovered family. As far as she was concerned, that wasn't what she was doing. Eleanor intended to come back to him, to mend what was torn, if he would allow it. But looking at him now, she didn't know if he would. Clearly Viggo was not the forgiving type.

He was so angry with his own family that he abandoned civilized life completely and took up residence in a cave. What would he do to evade Eleanor if he decided her visit to Yore was unforgivable?

Packing her things was a quick task. Her handful of dresses were still stuffed in a sack from yesterday. She had no keepsakes besides the ring Viggo gave her. Would he want it back? Did he consider this goodbye?

Her heart felt clipped at the thought and her movements stuttered. So quickly she'd fallen in love with him. Would he discard her just as quickly? The bond seemed to barely exist, quiet and hollow between them.

"This is not farewell," she whispered to him as he took her in his hand. "I wish only to know my family."

The flight was cold and quick. When Viggo dropped her near the city wall, he turned as if to leave immediately.

"Wait!" She yelled to his back. "I love you. Please don't forget that, even if you choose not to forgive me."

He glanced over his wings at her, then pushed up into the air. The emptiness inside of her grew and for the first time, Eleanor reconsidered. Was meeting a family of strangers more important than him?

No. She couldn't think of it that way because it was not so simple. She didn't have to choose between them. It was he who was being stubborn, refusing to understand her needs. In the end, it was selfish of him. Eleanor should not feel remorse for seeking what she wanted.

But just because she shouldn't feel something didn't mean she wouldn't.

Over the past two months, Eleanor felt as if she was ripped from her life and tossed into a strange and thrilling dream. First there was finding Viggo, now she was being bustled through the castle and welcomed by the royal family of Brula. Compared to her days with Viggo this was so jarring that her head twirled as a series of clucking servants led her from one room to another.

Their first visit was to see the king himself. He chastised her for leaving the castle but was shockingly gracious to someone that had been scrubbing his floors not long ago. During their brief meeting he asked that she speak well of him to her parents and let them know that he would like to visit their kingdom in honor of her return. Eleanor nodded, hoping she would remember to do that when she was finally faced with the people who called her daughter.

Next Eleanor was brought to another guest chamber similar to the previous one. This time she allowed them to strip her of her own dress but only if she had say in what they chose for her. Unfortunately, each gown they offered was more hideous than the last. She ended up choosing some fluffy purple thing and regretting it when they began cinching up the back.

Most of the servants were polite to her, but more than one gave bitter scowls and whispered cruelly about her. Eleanor was familiar with many of their faces, though she didn't know them personally, and she imagined that it rankled to be treating her as a courtier when only weeks ago she'd been a lowly maid herself.

"Thank you," she was sure to say as often as she could. "Thank you for tending to me." If she was to be a princess, she should practice being gracious.

By the time she was at the docks, accompanied by the prince, his guards, and too many other people to count, Eleanor was grateful for the chaos. It kept her mind too occupied to think of Viggo and what he was doing. Unbidden her eyes lifted to the sky, as if she might see him soaring overhead, returning for her. It was a small blessing that Mikael was not at the prince's side. Eleanor didn't know if she could keep a straight face if she saw his too similar eyes.

"My lady." Jerome took her hands in his and met her gaze, looking far kinder than she knew him to be. "I wish you a safe voyage. Send your parents blessings from me personally and my family. We will meet again soon."

"Thanks." Eleanor tugged her hands from his and hurried to where a sailboat waited for her. Nerves were getting the best of her, and she wanted to get herself on the boat before she panicked and ran away.

This would have been so easy if Viggo were here. His confidence was so well worn that it became contagious.

A sailor showed her to private quarters in the belly of the ship while they loaded supplies. Apparently, the king had included gifts for the royal family of Yore, enough gifts that it took half an hour to carry them aboard. It wasn't a particularly large ship, and she found herself hoping the crates wouldn't sink them. She'd never been on a boat before and the subtle, constant movement of the water was unsettling. The sound of waves lapping beneath the window of her quarters wasn't reassuring either.

The journey from Brula to Yore was supposed to take a day with good winds. The first mate came to inform her that they were blessed with good weather and would be docking in time for dinner. Though she hadn't eaten anything but a nibble of cheese offered to her back at the castle, Eleanor's stomach soured at the thought of food.

That sour, sloshing feeling didn't leave for the entire trip. She spent the day lying on her side, one hand clutching her stomach as she tried not to look at the liquid landscape out the window. Perhaps it was the movement of the boat or perhaps it was the tightness of her dress that had her dizzy and ill.

Or perhaps it was the growing ache in her heart, the hollow pain that throbbed with every creak of the boat.

She was alone again. Viggo left her to this task on her own. And what if her new family didn't like her? What if they decided they didn't want her returned to them? Where would she go then? It seemed impossible to think she could return to the Winter Wilds after this.

It was very likely that her heart was breaking, and she feared it could not be mended. Finding her family wasn't supposed to make her feel so empty.

Eleanor woke with a start, the sudden rush of noises contrasting with the relaxing lull of the sea. Men shouted, boots thumped overhead, and loud bells were ringing.

A moment later a heavy hand fell on her door and the first mate announced, "We have arrived, my lady. They're expecting you!"

The urge to hike up her dress and jump through the window was strong. But the water was cold, and she wasn't sure she could swim in a dress. And really, her family couldn't be that bad. They were as eager to meet her as she was to meet them, she imagined.

With a deep breath for bravery, Eleanor patted down the frizz in her hair and exited the boat. She was still dizzy and disoriented from being on the water. The dock felt as if it was moving beneath her feet. She grabbed the arm of one of the sailors leading her forward, startling the poor man and nearly sending him into the water.

"I apologize," she whispered. "I feel strange."

"You haven't got your sea legs yet." He smiled kindly and steadied her until they were stepping onto a cobblestone road.

Eleanor was so fixated on her feet and not letting them stumble that she hadn't realized why there was so much noise. A murmur of voices filled the street before her and when she stepped off the docks, those voices rose to shouts. The jump in volume made her scream. Thankfully none but the chuckling sailors noticed.

The cobblestone road was brightly illuminated by lanterns that seemed to glow supernaturally. Flames danced inside of them, but they were white and strangely bright. Those flames made it possible for her to see from where she stood all the way up the hill, where the road snaked past businesses and homes to meet with the gates of an enormous castle wall.

And that castle—Gods it was huge. Brula was supposed to be larger than Yore, so she hadn't imagined the royal home would be this significant.

Towers jutted out on all sides, built of stones colored a deep shade of blue. Rather than ending in points as she was used to seeing, the tops of the towers were shaped like orbs. From here Eleanor could see lights glowing through massive windows carved into each tower.

The castle itself had a similar roundness to it, blue stone making up odd curves and edges. There was none of the cold harshness that the capitol of Brula embodied. Though Yore was as cold and frosty, the surrounding city felt warm. Welcoming.

It helped that there were hundreds—maybe thousands of people on either side of the road, cheering.

"The princess has returned!" They called. "Elisa! Princess Elisa!"

"My name is Eleanor," she whispered into the racket.

A white carriage appeared on the street. The round shape of it reminded her of an onion on wheels. It was pulled by two magnificent horses, their coats so white they could have been specters. Eleanor was frozen in an awed daze as the carriage pulled up beside her and a set of red-carpeted stairs dropped down the side. The driver jumped from his perch and rushed around the side of the carriage, standing stiffly with his hand outstretched as a small man in white furs stepped from the carriage.

His furs glittered blue in the lights above them as he descended the stairs. There were sapphires embedded in his clothing, big blue gems to match the ones that decorated his heavy crown. Eleanor wanted to look to his face and search his features for some familiarity, but she was blinded by the extravagant display of wealth. A woman stepped out after him, her gown and fur cloak decorated in much the same way. The crown she wore was simpler and lighter, but no less sparkly.

The king made a show of looking her up and down, clasping his hand over his mouth as if startled by her appearance. Eleanor didn't know if it was horror or surprise that made his eyes widen.

"Elisa!" He hissed, stepping toward her with outstretched hands. "Gods have mercy on me. I can't believe you stand before us now."

She accepted his offered hand, closing the distance between them. It was a soft hand, much softer and more delicate than hers. They stood facing each other, no words exchanged, the expressions on his face indiscernible to her.

"Come, Iva. Come look upon our daughter."

The queen approached, dabbing at her eyes with a handkerchief, though they were dry, and she clearly wasn't shedding any tears. Eleanor expected that her mother at least would embrace her—even Grandmama had offered a hug once or twice a year—but she only took Eleanor's hand and squeezed lightly before quickly releasing her.

In unison the king and queen turned to the people gathered in the streets, leaving space between them for Eleanor to be seen. She found herself with the urge to run again, to dive off the docks and into the water if that was what it took to get some of the eyes off her. Being the center of such rapt attention from so many people was uncomfortable.

"People of Yore!" The king boomed, sending an immediate hush over the excited crowd. "The gods have blessed us so. The Hope of Yore has been returned to us!"

The people raised their arms to the sky and cheered again, chanting, "The Hope of Yore!"

The Hope of Yore? That sounded...important. Eleanor hadn't considered what kind of responsibility they might expect her to take on as a princess. She'd only considered meeting her family. Perhaps this was what Viggo was concerned with.

"Join us, daughter. Your brothers are waiting to dine with you." The king gestured to the carriage, stepping back in and seating himself on a plush bench. He was quickly followed by the queen, leaving Eleanor to waver on the cobblestone road.

What did it mean if she climbed into that carriage? What future awaited her in that beautiful blue castle?

The queen—*her mother*—smiled encouragingly at her from her shadowed perch inside. Eleanor exhaled and accepted the driver's hand as she carefully climbed the steps.

Now that she was truly seeing her, the queen was beautiful. Breathtakingly so. Her hair was a golden blonde, her eyes a cerulean shade of blue that shined even brighter surrounded by her many sapphires. Each of her features was delicate and soft, feminine but perfectly defined. Eleanor thought she saw the faintest resemblance between their lips—she definitely had her mother's small nose—but she could see little else they shared. Even her hands were larger and more masculine than her mother's, her height more lanky and less willowy.

Perhaps she gained most of her looks from her father. Though, he bore none of her freckles and his hair was a dark shade of blonde rather than her washed out red. His chin jutted out a bit too far and his cheeks were tight, a strange contrast to the loose skin on his neck. For such a dazzlingly dressed king, she expected someone more handsome. Someone more...charming.

The steps were returned to their place inside the carriage and the door was shut. The king banged his fist against the roof of the carriage three times, and they began moving with a jolt.

"Your ship was late," he said plainly, glancing from her to the window where people were passing in a blur.

"The captain said the weather was favorable." She didn't want the sailors to be treated as if the arrival time was their fault.

The queen slumped against the bench. "Don't act as if you weren't pleased to occupy yourself." Her words were surprisingly venomous.

"I told you I was attending to matters of trade."

"Trading your seed with some kitchen girl's tongue," the queen muttered quiet enough that Eleanor didn't imagine she was meant to hear it.

Was this…was this truly how her parents would welcome her home?

"I see you inherited your aunt's unsightly freckles. Her hair too. That woman just can't keep out of our business." The queen plucked at a lock of Eleanor's hair and dropped it as if it was something dirty. "Never mind that. At least it proves you really are Elisa. We can cover the freckles. Perhaps the apothecary will have something to fix hair color as well."

Eleanor's tongue hovered frozen between her teeth. After another stretch of tense silence, she finally blurted, "I don't even know your names."

"Of course, daughter. How could you?" The king smiled blandly. "King Lars Eklund the third. You were named after my mother." When the queen made no attempt to introduce herself, he added, "And your lovely mother is Iva. You'll have to forgive her. It has been a troublesome time for us all. Learning that you might be alive, not knowing if it was truly our daughter, has brought about old pains." He leaned forward and briefly touched her knee. "And you, Elisa, are the Hope of Yore. You will bring a great age of prosperity to our kingdom."

"I don't know anything about money." This was already feeling like too much pressure. How could she be anyone's hope if they didn't know her?

"I've already arranged for you to begin studies," her mother assured. "King Brennard warned us of where you were found and that it would take quite a lot of work to civilize you."

Eleanor was quiet the rest of their short journey to the castle. When she thought of reuniting with parents she never knew, there were many more hugs and happy tears in her imagination. The woman seated beside her was distant, each of her words sounding more bitter than the last.

She also hadn't considered that being a princess by birth would mean that they actually expected her to behave as one. Her plan was to return to Viggo when she had her fill of her family, occasionally visiting when she finally convinced him to stop being a stubborn mule and come with her.

Now she was beginning to worry they wouldn't so easily let her leave. Clearly, they believed her to be important, if not to them then to their kingdom. What was Eleanor to do if they wouldn't allow her to return home?

What would Viggo do if he believed that she decided to stay?

Being here should have lessened the burden on her heart. Instead, Eleanor felt more lost than she'd been in her entire life. In less than two days she'd become a different person. A stranger.

How was she to be anyone's hope when she couldn't even give herself any?

CHAPTER 14

Eleanor

Eleanor had two brothers. Two older brothers that were indifferent to her arrival. Timit was the eldest, and he was polite, at the very least. Sampson rolled his eyes as the king gave another brief speech about hope and prosperity.

"Why should I be thrilled? She's not my sister, she's a stranger," he exclaimed, digging into his roast duck without waiting for the rest of them to sit.

She could hardly hold it against him. Sampson was right. Eleanor was a stranger in an ostentatious castle full of strange people. Dinner with her so-called family was awkward and tense. They spoke few words to her, mostly speaking of her and the impending visit from the royal family of Brula. Eleanor remembered then to mention King Brennard's message.

Her father winked in response and promised, "I will take very kindly to the King of Brula. He and I have an old arrangement to debate."

That was the last anyone addressed her at dinner. The food was likely the most expensive and fancy food she'd ever eaten, but it tasted bland and dry in her mouth. She felt invisible at the table, no different from the extra chairs and place settings. Useful when needed but otherwise ignored.

Was this why Viggo so vehemently opposed her coming here? Was he more familiar with the royal family of Yore than he let on? How could he have known she would be treated so coldly?

Each time she thought of Viggo became more painful than the last. He was shutting her off from his end of the bond, locking her out from any hint of emotion. Eleanor missed him terribly and the absence of their new bond was an ache.

After the meal, Eleanor was led to a chamber fit for...well, for a princess. Not unlike the one in Brula, there were fluffy, silk cushions everywhere. Blue wool curtains fluttered with the hurried movements of several servants as they dressed down the bed and prepared night clothes for Eleanor. It took quite a lot of insistence to get them to leave and let her dress herself. She would never grow accustomed to being fussed over like a child.

That was hours ago. So many hours that predawn light was seeping through an opening in the blue curtains that covered her windows. Beneath her the bed was soft. The blankets, stuffed with feathers, were warm. A fire crackled lazily in the hearth. None of it was comforting. None of it helped to ease her uncertainty.

Eleanor wasn't cut out to be a princess. One night with her family made that clear. She didn't have the beauty of her mother, nor the poise and grace expected of her.

And that was what she would tell them. She was so pleased to have found them and wished them well. Perhaps she would return for the summer solstice, once Viggo and she were wed.

If he will still have me.

Of course, he would, Eleanor assured herself as she flipped back the blankets and searched for something other than that hideous purple dress to wear. He said the bond between them was indelible. Surely, he wouldn't—couldn't—simply forget her because she sought out her only family.

Her thoughts were interrupted by a sudden flurry of activity. The bedroom door burst open, more women than she could count bustling into the room. Her mother was leading the charge, her hair perfectly braided atop her head, her icy blue gown pressed to perfection.

"You're still abed? Goodness, girl! Hurry now. Madam Perfurie does not tolerate tardiness."

"Madam who?" Eleanor asked as two servants spun her toward the large wardrobe, stripping her night dress as they went. A third girl appeared from nowhere, combing through the snarled hair that Eleanor forgot to braid.

"Your etiquette teacher. I can't go around introducing a commoner as a princess. You must learn to behave properly."

Eleanor scowled, making her arms rigid so the dress sleeves they were trying to force over her couldn't slide further. "You've no idea if I've got manners. Grandmama taught me to mind my elders and give my thanks."

The queen scoffed. "That hag was not your blood. I won't argue with you, Elisa."

"Eleanor," Eleanor muttered, yielding her arms and allowing the servants to finish with the too blue dress they were lacing up. "My name is Eleanor."

Madam Perfurie was more than intolerant of tardiness. After being rushed down a maze of hallways and shoved through a set of great oak doors, Eleanor was immediately met with the sting of a switch across the back of her hand.

She recoiled, shaking the damaged appendage and snapping, "Gods, what is wrong with you woman?"

"You're late. And speaking out of term." Madam Perfurie raised the switch for a second blow.

Eleanor dodged, slipping around the long table and yanking out a chair. "Are we to dine together? I'm famished."

"You will mind your tongue, girl. A princess is to be seen not heard."

Apparently, Eleanor was uncivilized. At least, that was what half an hour with Madam Perfurie led her to believe. The way she held her fork, her head, and her tongue were all wrong. Each time she made a mistake, Eleanor was swatted. Both her hands were pink and burning. She hadn't been allowed to take a single bite yet.

Her stomach growled unhappily, and she clenched her fork.

"Not that one!" Madam Perfurie squawked, raising her switch threateningly.

The swish of that Gods awful switch was still ringing in her ears when Eleanor exited the small dining hall at the end of her lesson. Her stomach was painfully empty, and she hadn't successfully accomplished any of the tasks put to her by her etiquette teacher. Manners and court etiquette were not the same thing, she was realizing, and one would likely cause her to starve to death.

Three steps were barely taken into the hall before one of her many new servants appeared. Eleanor was dragged from one lesson to another, dropping into a chair in the library and barely catching her breath before a stuffy old man began lecturing her.

Reading was no easier than etiquette, though that was probably due to her hunger. How was she to concentrate on an empty stomach?

"A princess should be well spoken and well read," her tutor reminded when Eleanor lost focus while fantasizing about bread.

A princess was to have a lot of qualities that Eleanor did not possess. Etiquette and education would not improve her personality.

One day quickly became three. Three was a fortnight before Eleanor knew it and there was no chance to plan a trip home. Her days were too busy, too overfilled with boring, bitter people that she had absolutely no interest in spending her time with. The only chance she had to see her parents, or her brothers was when they dined together every evening.

Conversation was dull, and no one was interested in engaging with her. More often than not the queen was sniping at the king for one offense or another. They did not appear to trust each other, nor did they like each other. Eleanor had never fathomed that life in a royal family could be so miserable. She found herself feeling a new sense of compassion for Viggo.

He couldn't choose his family any more than the rest of them could. The sole escape he saw from this life was extreme. Total abandonment of his family and everything they stood for. It wasn't that he didn't love them, only that he couldn't support their way of life.

Eleanor was beginning to feel much the same about her parents and she'd only known them two weeks. Insufferable, lazy, and too wealthy for their own good. For the leaders of a country, they cared far too little about anything of importance.

Her breaking point came late into the third week. She was sick of heart, hungry, and downright tired of leaving the dining hall with damaged hands.

Madam Perfurie was mean and abusive. Eleanor paid her back in kind.

"Chin up!" Her shrill voice demanded. "Soft hands, girl. *I said soft!*"

The switch flew violently toward the back of her hand. At the last moment, Eleanor flipped her palm up, grabbing the tip of that awful stick and yanking. Madam Perfurie was a slight woman, easily overpowered by hands as rough and used as Eleanor's.

"You are a vile woman!" Eleanor snarled, raising the switch and whacking Madam Perfurie repeatedly.

The woman covered her face, crying out and stumbling back. Eleanor did not yield until she had fallen onto her rear, her dress puddling around her. With one final flick Eleanor snapped the switch in half and tossed it to the floor. Then she grabbed as many rolls and handfuls of bacon as her hands could get, stuffing them into her mouth as she made her exit.

With a mouth full of food, she tossed her parting words at Madam Perfurie. "I would rather be uncivilized than spend another minute with the likes of you."

Bacon grease dripped between her fingers as she marched back to her chambers. Eleanor licked it greedily, sating her hunger for the first time in weeks. The single dinner she was provided every night was not enough to fill her belly and she felt as if she was starving to death. Even during the harshest Brulian winters, Eleanor had not gone so hungry. Apparently, her mother believed a princess should be trim.

"A princess will be whatever she pleases," Eleanor grumbled, dropping onto the end of her bed and staring at her filthy hands. The place on her finger where Viggo's ring should have sat was uncomfortably naked. She'd taken to wearing it on a chain tucked into her bodice. Otherwise, her mother made such a fuss. They didn't believe her when she asserted she was engaged. Where was this groom she claimed to have?

Where, indeed?

More than once, she'd begun to wonder if she would ever see him again. Viggo felt more of a ghost that was haunting her mercilessly than a lover aching for her return.

She was almost as angry with him as she was longing for him. Didn't he miss her the way she missed him? Or was it all another game to him, a playful dalliance to add more pleasure to his already hedonistic life?

"Elisa!" Her pondering were interrupted by her mother's piercing voice. The queen barged into her chambers, the cloud of servants that constantly orbited her filling the room and busying themselves with tasks they'd already been given. "What have you done?"

Eleanor lifted her chin. "Spoken up for myself. That woman is a witch, and I will not be treated like some misbehaved cart horse." It was the first time she dared speak back to her mother and she could tell by the ashen color of the queen's face that it was not a good idea.

"The royal family of Brula is arriving tomorrow. *Tomorrow!* Do you know how important it is for you to make a good impression? You must appear the well-bred princess that you are. I will *not* have you embarrassing us."

"I cleaned the Brulian King's privy for years! He knows me as a dirty servant girl that scrubbed floors and tended to his spoiled son."

The queen raised her hand and smacked Eleanor across the face. When Eleanor lifted her head in shock, her other cheek was given the same treatment. All around them, the bustle of maids and servants had ceased, each girl frozen in time as they waited with bated breath to see what would happen next. "You ungrateful, useless creature. It's bad enough that you come to us used and cover in those dreadful marks. You are never to speak of the prince that way again. Do you understand me? He is your greatest prospect and a marriage to him would mean everything for this kingdom."

Ha! Marry Jerome? He wouldn't want to marry her anymore than she would want him. "I'm already engaged."

"To a groom that clearly doesn't want you." That burned far worse than her mother's slaps. "Enough of that nonsense. You're to try on dresses and you will not fuss. Everything must be *perfect* tomorrow, including you."

Eleanor wanted nothing more than to be left alone. Instead, she was poked and prodded. Stripped and redressed and stripped again. She wasn't particularly unhappy with her body—though her ribs and hip bones were becoming quite prominent on her single meal diet—but she wasn't keen on displaying it for a bunch of strangers either. The servants were circumspect enough as they measured her and tied fabrics around her waist. Mother was not.

"Your hips are too thick. She'll need a dress that accentuates the bust more than the waist." The queen waved to one of the girls who hurried over with another dress. "And where is that girl with the makeup? I want to ensure not a mark will show when she's finished." Another servant rushed over, opening a heavy box and pulling out tins of pale powders. "Get to it then. I want each of her freckles gone. And that Gods awful birth mark too. What is that?"

Eleanor glanced down to see the queen pointing to the pale blue mark over her left breast. Viggo hadn't been able to explain its appearance beyond "magic," but she was fairly certain it served the same purpose as the ring he gave her. It was *his* mark, his claim to her as a bride.

All dragon brides had them, according to him. Hers was small, no larger than a gold coin. A beautiful blue reptilian body curling in on itself. From a distance it almost looked like a tangle of veins and since it was impolite to study a woman's breasts, she could understand why her mother might find it strange. That didn't mean she was going to capitulate.

"No." She placed her hand over the mark. "You can't cover it."

"Elisa, that is one of the ugliest birth marks I've ever seen. It will be covered or else your bust will be hideous. Those breasts are too small as it is. Don't make it worse! We have to find *some* way to make you enticing to the prince's gaze."

Her protests fell on deaf ears, so Eleanor stopped fighting. She was a doll to them. One girl smeared powders all over her face and chest while another combed a strange brown paste into her hair. When they were finished hours later, Eleanor didn't recognize herself.

Dressed in a gown to match the sapphire colored walls, she was the perfect decoration. Her skin was a pale, pale white, her freckles and Viggo's mark nowhere to be found. The most jarring change to her appearance was her hair. It was still damp from whatever they'd done to it, but even drying she could see the color was changed.

Brown. They'd made her hair brown.

All her life, Eleanor hated her hair. Each time she was teased she would pray to the Gods to make it change. Let it choose one solid color instead of that strange washed-out red. But she'd learned to be comfortable in herself over the years. Recently she'd even gained a certain confidence. Now it was destroyed, tucked away with all the other parts that made up her. Eleanor had become something and not someone.

The queen stood behind her in the mirror, smiling as she put hands on Eleanor's shoulders. Her words were not nearly as kind as anticipated. "That will have to do. Only a witch could make you pretty and even we don't have that kind of wealth."

Then they were gone. The queen trotted off, taking her hens with her.

Eleanor stared into the mirror until her eyes watered. She'd never felt so defeated before—so defeated and so very alone.

CHAPTER 15

VIGGO

S ELF-LOATHING WAS NOT A new feeling for Viggo. When he opened his eyes and realized what kind to man he was growing into, what kind he was expected to be in his family if he took his father's role, he hated himself. He hated his life and upbringing and all the people around him. But mostly himself. It was he who allowed such behavior to continue without judgement.

Somehow, he'd forgotten that blame during his years in the wild. He'd forgotten how to take responsibility. Once again, he'd become selfish. Just because it wasn't in the same vein as his brother and the other nasty men at court didn't mean that it mattered less.

It mattered more because it had cost him dearly. Eleanor was gone and Viggo was completely at fault.

At first, he'd been angry with her, so angry that he cut her off from their bond. But he still felt everything from her. Trepidation, disappointment, heartbreak.

Heartbreak. That was his fault too.

He expected that being thrust into the role of a princess—even if she truly was this Elisa—would not be good for her. Now he was feeling firsthand how true that was. But would she be suffering so if only he'd gone with her? If he had chosen to look beyond his own biases, he could have shielded her from the worst of it. She knew nothing of that world except from what she learned serving it. Court politics were not easy to navigate for a humble maid.

For weeks, he refused to see it. He took to the skies, hunted, soaked, and did only what brought him pleasure. What *pleased* him. Why not, if his mate would leave and do the same?

Foolish. Selfish. Arrogant. He was a terrible man and Viggo was ashamed of himself.

He'd been so eager to be a victim to his parents, too. They wanted him to marry regardless of his mate, wanted him to learn a role he wasn't suited for. Had he ever tried to make them see reason, or had he behaved like a petulant boy and gone off to drink and party and waste his days? Then, when his father finally put his foot down, Viggo left. He packed a small satchel and vanished into the wilds. It was liberating, but it was also juvenile.

Until Eleanor left, he hadn't been willing to admit that. Viggo refused to see anything but how wronged he was by what he was born into. But weren't so many wronged by their parents? The Gods? Fate? His mate lived a life much harder than his own and she hadn't whined and pitied herself. She abandoned it only when she saw no other option for herself.

Eleanor was braver than he. Perhaps he didn't even deserve her.

He needed her, though. As his anger died down to embers, he felt nothing but emptiness in its place. He could spend another twenty years playing at outcast in his cave and it would never fulfill him the way building a future with her would. Eleanor pushed him to reconsider himself. She highlighted his flaws—not unkindly—and forced him to face them. To fix them.

She made him want to be a better man, not out of guilt, but because he realized that he was capable of so much more.

But only if she was there to witness it.

So Viggo did the unthinkable. When he'd finally had enough of being alone, of longing for her touch, he took to the skies and travelled east of Brula to his parent's cliff side home.

He was greeted with uncertainty, both parents too afraid to embrace him lest he flee for another decade or three. Viggo saved them their worry by wrapping an arm around them both and explaining, "I've decided its time to come home."

He was not technically being a better man by coming home. Nor was he making amends. Viggo needed an opportunity to see El without ambushing her and he knew his family could provide it. So, truthfully, this was a dishonest scheme. He didn't intend to inherit his father's duties as lord, and he certainly wasn't going to entertain his mother's plans to marry him to a suitable girl. But he would play his part when his family boarded a ship with the royal family of Brula and travelled to Yore to meet the princess returned.

Then he could make his amends. Perhaps he was too harsh on his family. That didn't mean he could ever return to them. They were pompous and suffocating and he had grown too wild for their way of life. This was what Eleanor wanted, though, so he would sacrifice that wildness for as long as it took to win her forgiveness.

"Thank the Gods. I knew you would return to us," his mother whispered tearfully into his chest. Before he could get a word in, she added, "I've been arranging matches for you with the eligible ladies of Yore, just in case."

Viggo rolled his eyes heavenward.

For my sweet El, he reminded himself. *I'm doing this for her.*

E LEANOR

Eleanor avoided her reflection as she was painted and posed again the next day. Thankfully her mother was busy readying herself for the arrival of the Brulian royals and wasn't hovering around the room, throwing insults. With each stroke of the soft brush over her cheeks, Eleanor felt erased.

Grandmama was right, that wretched woman. They were using Eleanor as a piece in their game. They weren't happy to have *her* at all. She had to wonder why they hadn't just picked any woman who resembled the queen and chose her to be Elisa. The outcome would have been the same.

Her breasts were pinned up so high she could hardly breathe. Movement was proving to be limited as the heeled shoes designed to make her look slimmer wobbled under her feet. It took Eleanor what seemed like hours to reach the carriage waiting for her and her family in the castle courtyard.

No one spoke as they were stuffed into the giant onion. The ride to the docks might as well have been another dinner for all her brothers looked at her. Her mother too was absent, staring out the window with a pensive scowl. She only broke her concentration to swat at Eleanor's hand as she tried to bite her nails.

An evening pretending to be a princess was bad enough. An evening pretending to be a princess for the sake of *Jerome* and his ilk would be nauseating. And Viggo would be furious.

If he still cares.

The insecurity made the ring on her finger feel heavier. She glanced down at her act of rebellion, smiling privately at the sapphire that gleamed back at her. Perhaps he didn't care, but she did. So very much. And even if they covered her mark, she wanted the court to know that she belonged to Viggo. There would be no potential suitors. Not ever.

Thinking of him distracted her enough that she wasn't paying much attention to the fanfare as she was ushered from the carriage. Once again, the streets were lined with people. White ribbons stretched between lamp posts to celebrate their royal guests. The ship stationed at the dock was much fancier and better built than the one that brought Eleanor. She imagined it was filled with as many ridiculous throw pillows as all the rooms in the Brulian castle.

King Brennard and his wife were in the lead, but they were closely followed by Prince Jerome. Not far behind him were several lords and their wives. One she recognized as Lord Nordin. Viggo's father. The man that would have been her father-in-law someday. They shared height and coloring, though Viggo was paler and more pointed than his father. Mikael was next, signature sneer spreading his lips. There was one more man behind him, as tall and elegant as the rest...

Eleanor gasped, tripping on her stupid wobbling shoes and bumping into her brother. He gripped her arm to steady her, causing her to collide with her other brother. Both were glowering down at her, but she paid them no mind.

How could she when Viggo was coming down the docks? His hair was braided down the center of his scalp, the sides of his head sheared clean. Everything about him was elegant and masculine. His sharp jaw was clean shaven, his clothing the finest she'd ever seen him wear. The dancing dragon crest on his breast completed the look. He was a future lord. She saw it. For the first time she saw how truly regal he was.

The roaring in her ears kept her from hearing whatever it was the King of Brula said. Most of the exchanged pleasantries went unanswered by her as she struggled to fathom why Viggo was here. Even more struggle was keeping her eyes off him. Every inch of him was perfect. The magnetism was not mutual, it would seem. He scarcely offered her a cursory glance before letting his mother lead him away.

Eleanor was not the only one to notice Viggo's allure. After an endless, bumpy ride back to the castle, she was immediately shoved into the middle of a bustling party. Courtiers she'd never met tried to speak to her of topics she didn't understand. Each time her gaze snagged on Viggo, she saw another woman flailing her hands around him, blushing and giggling like a fool. To his credit, Viggo was paying them no mind.

Eleanor scurried away from the crowd as soon as she could, facing one of the massive windows and staring down at her cage of blue. He was here. *Viggo was here.* Why *now?* She breathed as deeply as her dress would allow, cursing the wretched stitches that held in her diaphragm.

There was no warning to announce his arrival. His footsteps were silent, his movement subtle and smooth. Eleanor didn't realize Viggo was standing beside her until he took her hand, bowing slightly and murmuring, "Princess Elisa, an honor."

"My name is Eleanor, as you very well know," she snarled, trying to yank her hand away.

"El, then." He held firm, bringing her knuckles to his lips. She'd nearly forgotten the heat of him, how even that simple brush of a kiss could warm her to the bone. "You look more a doll than a person."

She eyed his extravagant clothes. "Well, you look like a barbarian wrapped in silk."

That delicious purr of a laugh left his throat, and she wanted to hate him for how perfect of a sound it was. "I see being a princess has not improved your manners."

"What are you doing here?" Eleanor fixed her eyes back out the window, crossing her arms over her chest to guard her heart. She couldn't take any more heartbreak.

"I came to see you."

Her breath wanted to come too quickly but somehow, she held herself together. "Here I am."

"I also came to apologize." That turned her head so fast her neck cracked. "I made a mistake, Eleanor. A selfish, cruel mistake. It has cost me everything."

"Has it? I couldn't tell."

All at once the bond whipped back open, every ounce of him pouring into her. She was hit with a heartbreak so fierce it could have knocked her off her feet. The only reason she withstood it was because she had grown accustomed to it; his heartbreak matched her own.

There was more, too. Longing, loneliness, regret rooted so deep it could rival all the bonewoods in the Winter Wilds.

"It has."

"Viggo…" A single tear slipped down her cheek.

Viggo caught it, brushing the moisture into her carefully painted face and ruining the mask that hid her freckles. "No tears, El."

"I have missed you so terribly. I feared I would die from the ache of it."

"I'm sorry, sweet El. So very, very sorry."

Though she wanted nothing more than to fall into his arms, Eleanor held herself back. A simple apology wasn't enough. "Prove it."

He chuckled, his eyes sparkling the way they always did when they looked upon her. "Eleanor, I was so determined to mend what I've broken that I returned home to my family. I've spent hours wearing this Gods awful costume. I even spoke polite words to Jerome and his father. If I was any sorrier, I would throw myself from the balcony."

"Go ahead. Throw yourself. Such a hollow gesture from a man who can grow wings." But she was smiling when she said it, her chest feeling light for the first time since she'd left Brula.

"Mistress of my heart, you are so cold."

"Too many nights in a winter cave has iced over my own heart."

"I believe I know the remedy to that."

They quieted, staring at each other as if it was the first time. Viggo could be so mercurial, and she loved him all the more for it. He was here. He was here *for her*. Eleanor was not going to struggle to forgive him.

"I hate being a princess," she finally admitted.

"You don't have to be."

Viggo's mother chose that moment to interrupt, appearing out of nowhere and gripping Viggo's arm. "Viggo, you're not involving yourself in the party. Come meet the eligible ladies of the Yore court."

Jealousy reared up inside of Eleanor so fast that she had to restrain herself from wrenching Lady Nordin's hand away from Viggo. She was a dragon bride. How could she push her son on just any woman, knowing the connection that he could—he *did*—have with his mate? Unbelievable.

"Ah, Princess Elisa. You are as lovely as your father claimed. Please excuse my son."

Viggo opened his mouth to protest but whatever words he planned to speak were interrupted when Eleanor's mother arrived with the queen of Brula in tow. They were babbling on about summer weddings and colors and all sorts of boring topics, dragging Eleanor into it as if she cared.

The night went on like that. Viggo pulled to one end of the room, Eleanor to the other. If she didn't know any better, she would suspect that Viggo's mother was trying to keep them apart. Each time Eleanor excused herself from one conversation, another courtier rushed in to get her attention. Why they bothered speaking to her, she couldn't say. Her skills had not improved during her lessons, and she stumbled over every word as her attention fixated on a stray female hand caressing Viggo's arm.

Eleanor was about to remove that hand from whatever arm it belonged to when she was ushered into the dining hall and all but forced into her seat. Her mother, it would seem, noticed her absentmindedness and was not pleased.

"The prince is here for your company, Elisa. Be a good host." It was spoken in a sing-song voice, but it sounded more like a threat.

Jerome took the seat next to her, that ugly, charming smile plastered across his face. "Elisa, you are a vision."

"You give me visions, too." Visions of tossing the contents of her wine cup in his face.

"Don't tell me you're angry with me, Elisa." He put his hand over hers.

She removed her hand and placed it on the butt of her butter knife. "How could you tell?"

"Elisa, you must understand. You and I have been meant for each other from the day you were born. How was I to resist you?"

"Me and every other maid below the age of fifty that was foolish enough to believe you cared for them." She gripped the handle of the knife until her knuckles turned white. "Do not presume to speak to me again or my intended will eat you."

"I am your intended."

"Ha! Who told you that?"

Jerome leaned in close enough that she could smell his wine laden breath. "Careful, Elisa. Don't forget it was *me* who brought you to my father. If not for me, you would still be a filthy, flea-bitten maid, raising her skirt for any courtier willing to glance her way."

"You are not a prince, you're a pig."

A sudden hush fell over the hall. Eleanor glanced up to see her father standing at the head of the royal table, his cup raised. "I would like to propose a toast for the King of Brula. You have returned our hope to us and for that, we are eternally grateful." He shifted his hand to point his cup Eleanor's way. "Let us also drink to the future King and Queen of Brula. Lady Fate has seen fit to bring you back together after so many years." Cheers erupted around the table.

Confused, Eleanor glanced up and down. Her eyes found Viggo's, burning with fury as they locked on Jerome. Did he understand what was happening?

"Yes, it's true. I am pleased to announce that Prince Jerome and Princess Elisa are to be wed."

More cheers. Cups clinked together. Wine sloshed. Eleanor's ears buzzed from the noise, or maybe her pulse spiking. Beside her Jerome uncurled her fingers from her knife and raised her hand in his.

Eleanor jerked it away, standing so fast her chair tumbled back several feet. The cheering died in an instant, replaced by a bemused murmur.

"I've had quite enough!" She shouted, slamming her hand down on the table and sending several glasses spilling across the linens.

"Elisa!" He mother hissed.

"*My name is Eleanor!*" She snatched a napkin from the table, wiping the layers of powder from her face.

Finally, with her chin jutted out defiantly, she rubbed away more powder to reveal the blue mark over her left breast. Viggo's mother was the first to gasp, her eyes rounding as they took in the mark of a dragon bride. Her gaze fell heavily upon Viggo, and she scowled.

"You people are *terrible.* Truly, you are all so terrible. You lie and dally with your servants and speak words meant to wound. Gods have mercy on the subjects you rule."

"Elisa, what are you—"

Eleanor cut off her father's sputtering. "Viggo, I would like to go home now."

Viggo stood with smooth grace, his smile feline. "Whatever you wish, El."

"I—Lord Nordin, what is the meaning of this?"

Viggo's father was clearly torn. He understood what the mark Eleanor bore meant. There was no point in arguing with Viggo. "Your highness, I had no idea…"

"I *told you* that I was to be a bride, mother." She took Viggo's hand, breathing out a sigh of relief when they were joined again. "I cannot lie and say it was lovely to meet you. You're not very good parents. But perhaps you could be. We'll come visit in the summer. I'll send word."

With that Viggo led her away, rushing back into the party hall and to the open doors of the balcony. Cold air whipped at her hair and tussled her dress.

"It's a very long journey back to Brula and you are not prepared for the weather."

"So, don't take me back to Brula. Just take me anywhere that isn't here."

Viggo studied her face. Behind them, a cacophony of noise grew as the curious—or perhaps furious—crowd followed them from the dining hall. "Are you certain?"

"Absolutely certain."

"If it pleases the princess." He smirked, gripping her waist and hoisting her onto the railing. It was slick, and she nearly lost her footing when he let go.

"Viggo, what are you doing?" She should have realized as soon as they went for the balcony and not the staircase.

"Throwing myself off the balcony."

"You better catch me, dragon."

"I would never let you fall." Then he leapt over the edge.

"Elisa!" Her father's wrathful voice boomed behind her. "Get back here this instant!"

A gust of air buffeted her dress, temporarily blinding her as her hair covered her eyes. Eleanor caught one glance of her father's horrified expression moments before the talons of a dragon settled around her waist and she was rocketed into the night sky.

CHAPTER 16

Eleanor

Viggo had no clothing when they landed near a roadside inn outside of the capital of Yore. Eleanor had no money. The innkeeper was thrilled to accept her sparkling pearl earrings and the matching pearl necklace as payment, however. She even went out of her way to fetch a spare cloak for Eleanor's husband, who "fell in a puddle while trying to catch their errant horse." It was the worst lie she'd ever come up with, but the old woman was so fixated on valuing out the precious jewelry that she didn't seem to notice.

Thankfully, she also didn't notice Viggo's bare calves as he hurried up the stairs to their room.

The ceiling in the room was so low that Viggo nearly smacked his head. Even with a fire in the hearth the air was cold and damp. Worse was the hay stuffed bed, which would require Eleanor to sleep atop Viggo if they were both going to fit.

It was as far from the luxury her parents offered as she could get. For that, Eleanor was grateful. Besides, she wouldn't mind having Viggo under her.

Apparently, his thinking was following a similar trail. He was free from his cloak in a moment, his hands already working the threads cinching her gown closed. The garment took far too much effort to remove without destroying. More than once, he let out a frustrated growl, and she feared he would rip it and force them to both travel home naked.

When she was bared to him, Viggo turned her into the firelight and stepped away.

"Gods you are even more beautiful than I remember."

She met his gaze, holding in tears as she said, "I don't ever want to be a mere memory to you again."

"Never, Eleanor. I will keep you by my side so long as we both live." Viggo took her in his arms, his skin delightfully warm. "Marry me."

She held up her hand, which still bore the ring he gave her. Mother could cover her mark, but she would have had to cut Eleanor's finger off to remove her ring again. "I'm already to marry you."

"Tomorrow. As soon as we find a temple."

Eleanor giggled. "Do you think a priest will marry us if you walk in there naked?"

"Good point." He lifted her by the waist and laid her gently in the bed. "Soon, then. Marry me when we return home."

"Of course." She kissed him, desperate to be as close to him as she could. "But tonight, let's not worry ourselves with it. Tonight, I only need you close to me."

"Oh, El." Viggo spread her legs with his hips. "My sweet, sweet El."

That night he made love to her as if it was the very first time. Each touch they shared was reverent, every kiss a whisper of love. They'd only slept for an hour when the sky became grey with dawn. Eleanor cursed the thin curtains as gold light peppered her eyelids through the window, pestering her until she could no longer sleep, despite her exhaustion.

"I suppose we should plan for our journey home." She sighed, combing fingers through her tangled hair. The color was still foreign.

Hopefully whatever disgusting herbal paste her mother's servants painted her with would wash out.

"I'm sorry, El."

"I've forgiven you quite a few times. You can stop apologizing."

"No, I'm sorry that your family was not what you hoped them to be." Viggo took a lock of hair from her fingers and examined it. "Perhaps now you understand the complicated relationship I have with my own parents. I love them, but I can never conform to their standards."

A tear slipped out unexpectedly and Eleanor swore it would be her last for at least a year. "Yes, I think I do understand. I didn't realize a mother's love could be so...conditional."

"The courts breed a particular kind of coldness into women."

"And a particular kind of debauchery into men."

Viggo chuckled humorlessly. "That is a side effect of believing yourself to be greater than those around you. Power makes men into cunning, greedy creatures."

"I think I've had my fill, at least for now." Someday she might return to visit her parents. Or perhaps not. Eleanor knew them for a few miserable weeks. She owed them nothing, as they owed her nothing. "I would like to go home now."

"Me too." Viggo considered for a moment, glaring at his borrowed cloak. "Perhaps we should hurry and use the dawn to our advantage. I don't think I will be particularly inconspicuous in that."

In the end, Eleanor was forced to travel clutched in Viggo's arms with nothing but that extra cloak to keep her warm. It was a much shorter journey by dragon than by sea, but it was no less uncomfortable. The air that pummeled them from the nearby water was painfully cold. When they were finally making a descent, she was surprised to find her limbs had not turned to icicles and fallen off.

Viggo landed in a clearing, surrounded by grey, leafless trees. They were not like those found in the Winter Wilds. These were darker and smaller. Some still bore color in bursts of evergreen branches.

"Wh-where are we?" She stuttered, taking Viggo's offered hand when he returned to his two-legged form.

"Home."

He led her down a short trail through the woods, stopping when the forest opened to a glittering view of the sea. Sitting prettily on the shore was a lovely stone cottage, it's roof clean and new. There were two chimneys coming from the roof and though they were void of smoke, Eleanor could almost feel the warmth inside.

"What is this place?" She resisted the urge to rush to the door and barge inside. The sea breeze was excruciating on her already frigid face.

"I told you, it's home." Viggo barged in for her, holding open the door and motioning her inside.

Eleanor stalled in a small entryway, watching as Viggo moved to a hearth in the large kitchen and made quick work of a fire. She hurried over to it, placing her hands as close as she dared. Viggo wrapped his arms around her waist, warming her back as the fire did the same for her front.

"We are only a six-mile walk from Vannar. I've been told the soil is good for farming, if we wish to garden and raise animals. The sea is a wealth of food as well. Though, personally, I am not partial to seafood." He stepped away to pull back a curtain that covered one of the kitchen windows. "If I'm honest, I mostly picked the place for the view. It's lovely when the sun is rising." He gestured to a hallway beyond the kitchen. "And the space. It's plenty of space for us and the children."

She raised a suspicious brow. "Do you have children that you haven't told me about?"

"Our children." He smiled that devilishly charming smile. "All twenty-seven of them."

"I thought we agreed on twenty-eight."

"You will make a wonderful mother, El."

The hope felt dangerous to allow, but she entertained it anyway. "You're serious? You'll give up the cave and live like a civilized man? Grow a family?" A family of her own, one that she could define with Viggo.

"I've been a selfish, lazy man. I want to be deserving of my bride."

"You are!" She exclaimed, wrapping her arms around him and kissing every part of his face. "I love this home, and I love you."

"My dear, sweet El," he murmured.

"Now show me to the master bed. Your bride needs to be warmed."

"Speak your dreams and I will make them come true."

"I wish to live happily ever after." She leapt into his arms, dotting his neck with more kisses.

"Mmm." He caught her lips for a languid drink. "I can arrange that."

THANK YOU FOR READING!

Want more dragon shifters and fated mates? Start the next book in the series now:

Ready for another fast-burn dragon shifter romance? Join my newsletter and download a Dragon Brides novella with new characters and a standalone story.

Thank you for reading Birthright! Would you help get my books in the hands of more readers by leaving a review?

Also By

Dragon Brides Series

Blood Feud
Black Heart
Midnight Ruin
Birthright

Beasts of Barbeaux Bayou

Shroud of Exile

Silver Bullet Security

Relentless

ABOUT THE AUTHOR

Moira Kane is a paranormal romance author who prefers to write stories about the dragon that eats Prince Charming. Each of her books has magic and mayhem, but most importantly, a happily ever after.

When she's not writing, Moira can be found nose-deep in a romance novel or searching the woods for her reclusive husband. A Pacific Northwest native turned Midwest transplant, Moira is happily raising three feral children. Some of her other job titles include baker, tree-hugger, dog whisperer, mushroom enthusiast, and weird home-school mom.

Learn more about Moira on her website: https://moirakane.com/

Instagram: @moirawritesromance

TikTok: @moirawritesromance

www.ingramcontent.com/pod-product-compliance
Lightning Source LLC
Chambersburg PA
CBHW011431310726
48972CB00011B/3008